LEGACY *of* TRIAEGIS

THE LEGACY COMPENDIUM

SHAWN HOLLADAY

Order this book online at www.trafford.com
or email orders@trafford.com

Most Trafford titles are also available at major online book retailers.

Printed in the United States of America.

ISBN: 978-1-4907-4307-3 (sc)
ISBN: 978-1-4907-4309-7 (hc)
ISBN: 978-1-4907-4308-0 (e)

Library of Congress Control Number: 2014913492

Trafford rev. 01/20/2015

 www.trafford.com

North America & international
toll-free: 1 888 232 4444 (USA & Canada)
fax: 812 355 4082

DEDICATION

This, my first book, is dedicated to my friends and family,
Who supported me through the long process.
Thank you, everyone.
Bryan Holladay, Tracy Scott
Keith Holladay, Bree Scott
Xavier Duenas
Brittny Hicks, Kaydra Townsend
Erica Close, Peggy Stevens
Kara Howard
And everyone else.

...

PROLOGUE

I added this part for everyone who has been living under a rock for the past two eras or so. For everyone else who has some knowledge of our world of Nu'Diina, you could skip this whole part, but who knows—you might learn something. Our realm is known as Nu'Diina which is a word derived from an extremely ancient dialect, and I don't think anyone alive actually knows what it means anymore. Here in our realm there are five major continents among three oceans. The largest and most populated continent is Kaladiin'Aaiyyr, which is the largest of the five and contains a significant portion of this realm's population. Kaladiin'Aaiyyr is host to a number of different nations, all of whom usually maintain a steady peace among each other. The largest both in population and politically is the Kingdom of Adiin'Ayr, one of the most powerful kingdoms in the world. Adiin'Ayr is home to the majority of this realm's population and landmass. The kingdom has been ruled by the Gallad family for over six centuries. King Aiden Gallad and his wife, Queen Saia Karkand, have ruled over Adiin'Ayr for decades, and the entire continent has prospered ever since. Shortly before King Aiden Gallad ascended to the throne, the Kingdom of Adiin'Ayr was involved in a centuries' old war with the barbarian armies of Inuskard to the north. However, Aiden Gallad ascended to the throne. He ended the war and inevitably married into one of the most powerful ruling families of Inuskard, the Karkands. This created a lasting peace between the two nations in which both have prospered.

Now the nation of Inuskard is the nation that controls the colder environment in the north of Kaladiin'Aaiyyr. Inuskard is a nation of courageous warriors who are usually extremely misunderstood. Many people from other nations call them savage barbarians, but they are actually a devoted, honor-bound society of warriors. They have a king, but most power lies with the individual barons who control the nation's cities and fortresses. Inuskard is pretty harsh environmentally, with extremely cold winters and a large amount of snowfall. I hear it gets quite beautiful in the summer, but in winter it's pretty much just white. The alliance between Inuskard and Adiin'Ayr has never been stronger, and now the two even operate joint military operations. Inuskard uses Adiin'Ayr's political connections to trade with the greater world. Among the powerhouses of Kaladiin'Aaiyyr, Inuskard's military is among the most fearsome in the world.

The third major power in Kaladiin'Aaiyyr is the royal state of Tasavalsorae along the southeasternmost coasts. Tasavalsorae is a powerful principality led by High Princess Emily Saejjyn. Her family has controlled Tasavalsorae since before recorded history though it's not clear why. The Saejjyn family seems to be regarded almost as a religious deity among their citizens. If Kaladiin'Aaiyyr is the financial and political power and Inuskard is the aggressive military power on the continent, then Tasavalsorae is the magical hearth. Tasavalsorae is the heart of the Collegium, the most prominent military college in the world. The Collegium has academies all over the world but was started and holds its inner council in the Tasavalsoran capital of Tasavalshae. This is a nation devoted to magic without regard for any other nation or their beliefs. Now aside from the nations of the mainland, the desert principalities of Januus'Anub is still considered among the nations of Kaladiin'Aaiyyr. The subcontinent on which these principalities lie is a complete desert with no other environment preset. The desert princes who rule here control claims of the desert surrounding their coastal cities, but the majority of the subcontinent's landmass go unclaimed. This is primarily because the large majority of Januus'Anub is completely uninhabitable to any large-scale civilization. Out there, only small, nomadic tribes survive, moving from water to water. This land known for sand and gold is among the wealthiest of nations despite its small size. Below the continent of Kaladiin'Aaiyyr is Kaladiin'Ashaal, and there really isn't much I can say about this strange place. There is no known civilization that rules here and no known amount of population. Any expedition that ever ventured here ended with them disappearing into the jungles of the Voltha and never being seen again. Kaladiin'Ashaal contains three environments, the northernmost being a massive dark swamp called the Voltha. South of the swamps of the Voltha is the barren lands, which gave the continent the name "The Wastelands." These barrens aren't a desert of sand but are a wasteland of craggy stone and dry plains of red and orange. The continent stretches to the southernmost pole and gets cold and snowy from what I hear, though I have no desire to go that far north or south.

The second most populated continent and easily the second most important, considering that Kaladiin'Ashaal is pretty much a no-man's-land, is Chaeyuun to the far west. On the map it is the farther continent to the west and has often been called the land of the rising sun. The sun rises over the western sea and inevitably sets in the east over the eastern sea. I can remember the sun setting over the desert sea from Kal'Hinrathos. On Chaeyuun, the Chae Empire is pretty much the only major power. The Chae Empire controls over 90 percent of the continent's overall landmass, which makes it even larger landwise than Adiin'Ayr. Despite the massive landmass of the Chae Empire, the overall population is less than that of Adiin'Ayr by just less than half. The population density in Chae is low over most of the continent with most of it being farm territory. The Chae Empire's primary export is agricultural, supplying food to most of the mainland of Kaladiin'Aaiyyr. The Chae Empire's military is smaller than that of the Adiin'Ayr's but consists mostly of samurai, some of the most highly trained and disciplined soldiers in the world. The empire has long been ruled by the Ming Taa family, creating the imperial reference of the Ming Taa Dynasty. The only opposition on the continent is from a small nation far north called the Nagasukai Shogunate, a military nation set up after the rise of the Ming Taa Dynasty from their vanquished foes after they won the war for succession. The Shogunate is a small nation with a small military and will never be any kind of threat against the Chae Empire. The two are often bitter rivals, but it's a rivalry that hasn't seen conflict in a century.

The last major continent is far to the east and is located in the middle of the ocean equally as far from Kaladiin'Aaiyyr as it is from Chaeyuun. This continent, Valjjain, is a large and rather mysterious land that has been effectively sealed off since the dawn of human civilization twenty thousand years ago because of its self-imposed isolation. What vague descriptions are available describe it as a lush jungle environment with a harsh volcanic terrain somewhere within. Valjjain is home to the Aegis Empire, who controls the entire landmass, though there is no specific information on them. No ships are allowed to dock or come near land without being destroyed by Aegis naval vessels, and they conduct all trade with the outside world through protectorate cities, one in Januus'Anub, one in Kaladiin'Aaiyyr, and one in Chaeyuun. I know that they possess enough advanced technology to ensure that they can maintain military supremacy both on the seas and at their cities outside of Valjjain.

Chapter 1

Dance at Dawn

This is pretty strange, penning this to paper. I'm not used to writing down my story, and I'm not really used to anybody caring. Now I can understand many of you will believe this is all fantasy, but I can assure you it is not. Many still won't believe me, but for those who do, I want to tell it exactly as it was. I'm not really sure where to begin, so I guess I'll try and tell my story first. My name is Kya—at least I think it is, but nobody told me otherwise, so I take it that's a good sign. I mean there is no way to tell. I never knew either of my parents. For those who care, my sob story begins fifteen or sixteen years ago—I'm not really sure. My father, the bastard, split before I was even born. I like to hope that he died painfully. My mother, she died in childbirth so I never knew her. I was raised by the penniless rabble of Kal'Hinrathos in the Kingdom of Adiin'Ayr along the desert coasts of the southeast. I was raised by beggars, though I hear having a baby greatly increased what they got for years, so I repaid them for everything by now.

Well, that's my teary sob story, so let's move on. As it is I still live in Kal'Hinrathos under a certain employ. I, unlike the others, could never get into the standing around for hours asking for handouts. I needed to actually do something. So since I was old enough to walk and think on my own I've been a thief, and no, I'm not really proud of it—well, maybe sometimes. So I'm a criminal, a pickpocket living in fear of the law, but hey, I'm still alive which is more than can be said for many others in this world so . . . Well, here is my story:

The day that this whole unexpected, and at times a tad overwhelming, adventure started was a dry and hot day, a very hot day. Kal'Hinrathos is in a desert area, so we got a lot of them. I was doing the usual, mingling in the overcrowded streets of the city. On a good day I could make a good amount, as long as I wasn't greedy. I usually stole only a little from a lot of people. This day, however, was a very bad day, and I managed to get myself into some trouble. I had raided several purses for moderate bounty, most of which I gave to the impoverished citizens of Kal'Hinrathos. I often shared most of my earnings with the other poor and destitute. I guess that makes me a virtuous thief, but I did take pleasure in depriving the rich and arrogant of their coin. On this day, however, I managed to find someone who actually noticed my subtle action, which was an amazing feat in itself. This did make me have to run, fast. The man who had noticed was a soldier of some kind, obviously from the desert lands of Januus'Anub across the Agiian Sea, farther to the southeast. As I was reaching into his purse, he managed to catch my hand, but only after I got what I was reaching for—he wasn't that good. Nevertheless he did catch me. I was able to wiggle my way out of his grip and break for the run. I'm not sure if he was after me or not, and I didn't care. I was too eager to be elsewhere as quickly as possible, perhaps too eagerly. This overeagerness is the main reason why I got into real trouble that day, and I was sure it was the end.

I had been running for I don't know how long, seems like an hour. I don't know why I kept running. I could have stopped in an alley and could have been safe, but I just kept going. Unfortunately, I didn't and kept running and soon found myself in dangerous territory. I mostly kept to the western quarter of the city, where most of the travelers came from the Ayr Highlands toward the coast for trade with the desert lands of Januus'Anub. However, Kal'Hinrathos is a very large city and has many districts I do not dare venture into. One such district happens to be the western city slums. Not even I dare to go there. I tend to stay within the trade quarter and some of the more public quarters around it. The western slum, however, is often described as "the Yards" due to its dirtiness and its lawlessness. The district is well walled in, as it was part of the old prison, and guards virtually never go there. The buildings have long since been torn down, but the walls still stand, which is lucky. A few years ago, the riots got so bad that the Baron of Kal'Hinrathos chose to simply close the district off and deny them access to food and water every time they caused problems. So far it's worked. As you can imagine, without guards to patrol the district, powerful gangs have sprung up in their stead, offering "protection" for a fee. It so happens that the currently most powerful gang and I aren't on good terms. A few years ago I stole something they believed was theirs, and they hunted me ever since. They answer to some big warlord who used to run a bandit tribe out in the desert until a few years ago—not sure why he retired here. He now runs the Desert Dragons, who are not exactly my biggest fans, to put it lightly—they want me dead.

With my ill luck, I actually wandered past those gates and into their territory. I am not surprised there are many gates and walls throughout the city from its constant expansion over the years, and I took one too many. I actually backed into one of the mindless brutes, thus starting my endless trail of terrible luck. The idiot simply looked at me for a second with a blank and empty expression, proving my theory that their heads were empty. Naturally, my luck turned for the worse, and although he didn't recognize me, his friend did. The first goon was obviously just that—a goon. He stood something like six and a half feet and was built like a portable meat shield with the brain power to match. We stood for what must have been forever in the street, with dust and sand blowing everywhere. The street was wide here. More likely it was the prison courtyard due to the well in the middle. The street was flooded with carts both in use and broken. Here people seemed to be selling all manner of goods, from food to useless trinkets, which were probably stolen or fake. After the longest time, the second goon who recognized me approached for whatever reason. He was not like the first goon—he was actually kind of short, five one or so, but looked smart, or smarter at least.

"Hey, you little weasel, you won't squirm out of this one now!" The first thing he said that I could hear, though he did say something to the meat sack before that I couldn't hear probably 'grab her' for that's what it did. Now, I don't think of myself as short, but this guy's hands were bigger than my head. I could feel his hands crushing my shoulders to the point where I could barely breathe. At this point I figured I was dead— our history was way too colorful for them to let me walk. I had stolen from them in the past and always escaped, but I guess even my luck wears thin, or so I thought. But just as the meat sack and the little bastard who recognized me totally had me, the strangest thing happened—a stranger stood up for me.

The man was a giant but not like the brainless oaf that had me. He was also nearly six and a half feet and well built, but intelligent looking and well scarred from many battles. The man wore an armor, the likes of which I have never seen before; they looked strong but not massively heavy. The armor was built to fit so perfectly that it had no apparent weakness. His armor is hard to describe, but I'll try. To start, the armor was black, or least very close to black; it's hard to tell in the sun. His armor wasn't typical with hard plates and chain mail at the joints; instead, it was plates that fit perfectly with each other so it covers pretty much every part from the neck down. His armor seemed perfectly forged at strange angles, so much so that it drew attention—confusing, mesmerizing, hypnotizing. His shoulder pieces were just as strangely angled in maddening ways of dark metal with twisting designs of silver. The shoulder pieces were like metal blocks, which leaves a person blank and empty in thought, as they are drawn into the deep designs carved within the metal. The bulk of his armor was covered in these confusing angles and the deep designs of silver carved seamlessly into the metal. The armor was symmetrical on both sides, but other than that, there didn't appear to be any kind of pattern to the angles.

The metal was smooth and looked like it was made of a single piece of perfectly carved crystal. Now it took me some time to realize why his armor was designed this way, so I won't make you wait that long and tell you what I was told. Apparently, there is a pattern to the madness and a reason why his armor is designed this way aside from aesthetics. According to Kara the angles are designed that way so that when someone strikes his armor, their weapon can never find a flat surface to impact, deflecting off the angled armor instead. This reduces the force of any impact massively, as any strike will only slide off the angled armor and away. The smooth nature of his armor is crucial to ensure that any attack finds a frictionless surface to slide off of, which actually provides a substantial bonus in combat. From a distance all the angles blur together to create a frightening dark visage, but the angles become clear upon any kind of inspection. This actually makes sense, as I have heard of other applications of angular defenses. Kal'Hinrathos uses large metal triangles attached to towers and walls for siege purposes. Like his armor, whenever a catapult or trebuchet projectile impacts the triangle, it will slide along the metal's angle and skip across the wall instead of crashing into it. Though I have never heard of anyone taking the design concept this far before.

The armor appeared to be heavy but not as massive as other suits I've seen around or heard of, yet by his movements, I can tell the armor did not encumber him much at all. Despite its heavy look he moved in it as if it were light armor, maybe barely heavier than hard leather. I'm guessing by its extremely advanced design, this armor was stronger than any massive suit despite being smaller and more compact. His hair was black at the roots and gradually turned into white at the tips. He had some facial hair, which was black and well trimmed, more of a stubble really. His hair was messy, likely due to the oh-so-well-known helmet hair. He wore two long swords of identical size and design that matched the mad angled craftsmanship of his armor with their scabbard and hilt. His swords were strung on his back instead of along his belt. He approached with a solid stance and a glare that went through you.

"Leave her be," was all he said but his words were backed by his glare and his stance, both of which said something different, more like "try me." As it turns out, they did, which was actually kind of funny.

"Who the hell are you?" was the first brilliant reply to come to my captor's mind. He stuttered because of the man's appearance. The armored man continued his slow approach to us from across the courtyard. The large, dumb goon was still crushing my inside with his giant paws, and the small goon was trying to stare down the unidentified warrior. Upon seeing this newly developed situation, many other Desert Dragon goons began appearing in the plaza from almost everywhere. By time the reinforcements stopped arriving, there was some twenty or so heavily armed raiders surrounding the plaza. At this point everyone who didn't have a weapon was running in every direction to avoid the obvious incoming bloodshed. Of course the armored man didn't seem at all concerned about his outnumbered situation. Instead he kept his gaze on the short goon as he continued his slow and confident approach.

"Stop now and we could forget your unwise insults and let you live," the shorter man said, standing between me and the armored man. You could tell he was nervous as he looked around at his men, waiting for the action he knew was coming. The armored man stopped near the well in the center of the plaza, and it turned into an awkward standoff. I could see past the short man to the armored man smiling slightly in a sadistic way. I have no idea how long we stood there, but eventually one man rushed from behind the armored man and met a rather humorous end. The raider charged from behind, but the armored man obviously knew he was there and kicked his knee, grabbed his shirt, and dumped him down the well. A few seconds later there was an echoing crash and a wince from everyone, including me. At this point everyone started taking the armored man a bit more seriously as no one wanted to make the first move.

"Get him!" the short man yelled, thrusting his finger at the armored figure. It took several moments for anyone to take action, but eventually their training made them obey. They approached slowly in tactical groups of four, armed with a wide assortment of weapons. The first group had a spiked mace, a maul, a flail, and a one-handed axe. The axe man was the first to attack followed by the mace man while the other two waited for an opening. The armored man didn't even pull his weapon. Instead he pushed the axe man past and drew the man's dagger and slit the throat of the mace man as he attacked and pushed his body down the well. The maul man came from behind and swung; the armored man moved just in time for a miss. The maul hit the well and shattered a good section of the well's side, sending dust into the air from the dry well. The maul man had stumbled from his miss, and the axe man swung around first while flail man approached slowly. The armored man grabbed the axe from the axe man, pushing him head first into the well, throwing his axe at the flail man. The axe was buried handle deep in the guy's chest, knocking him backward to the ground. The maul man tried a second assault with his two-handed hammer with no more luck than the first attempt, less perhaps. The armored man dodged the second attack, stomping on the guy's arm, making him drop the maul and pushing him back. The armored figure stabbed the dagger he stole form the axe man right under his chin through his throat, severing the brain stem.

The fight lasted about a minute and a half; he attacked with unnatural speed and proficiency. The remaining raiders were too scared to even move. The armored man turned toward the short man and drew both of his thirty-inch blades and slowly walked toward him and me. Now, yes, thirty inches isn't all that long for a sword blade, but trust me, when dual wielding you don't need long swords. It's better to dual wield two shorter swords since dual wielding is all about speed and agility. The short man backed up out of fear.

"Let her go," he said once more. The raiders regrouped for another more organized assault, proving that they were capable of tactics. As the first man attacked with an axe he was stopped by a block with the left sword, and he decapitated the man with the other. The second rushed from the other side with a sword, only to have his arm lopped off by a left overhand swing from the left sword, and he finished it with a left overhand swing from the right sword. As the first attack lopped off the raider's arm, the second from the right sword sliced a devastating gash from the left side of the raider's neck to the right side of his body, under his arm. The third and fourth tried a joint attack with a mace and a spear while the rest lined up to die. The third with the spear charged from the right, where a single swing of the armored man's sword hacked the spear in half, sending him stumbling backward. The fourth man attacked from the left with the mace, but the armored man blocked with his left sword while slicing the spear. When the third man stumbled backward, he used his right sword while still holding his block, severing the lower half of his body, sending blood and organs flying about.

The rest of the fight was pretty gruesome; he seemed not concerned about actually killing people but just wading through them. He shredded through most of the raiders that assembled before the rest ran. His charge sent blood, limbs, and vital organs flying about, soaking the sand with bodies of the fallen, just for me. After his wadding through flesh with his blades, he finally reached me, the short guy, and the meat sack. The short guy backed up and tripped while the meat shield tossed me across the courtyard into some broken wagons—it really hurt. I was able to look up soon enough to see the battle between the dumb one and the armored man. It was interesting at least. The big man grabbed a massive sword and shield hidden inside a shop. The battle was massive. The bulk and warrior seemed not at all ready to die. The bulk made the first move, swinging his nearly six-foot-long, crudely forged sword and missing, destroying a wooden support beam that held up a small overhang from the wall over the shops. The destruction of one of these beams didn't bring the overhang down but made it shake. The bulk was attacking fast and hard while defending with his shield, which looked more like a metal manhole cover. The warrior was mostly just dodging his attack without any opportunity to actually attack back. It was starting to seem like the dumb brute might actually be winning.

However, the balance of power was radically altered, even surprising the brute and the short man. The warrior crossed his blades and engulfed himself in a deep red flame that glowed brilliantly. His blades glowed red with fire and heat, and even his eyes turned to a bright red. He then, in a single strike with both blades, shattered the brute's shield, sending heated shrapnel flying everywhere. The brute basically went flying backward, but the warrior wasn't done yet. He made one more rush, brandishing his blades. He swung with both swords glowing brightly with fire blazing off them. The brute tried to block with his sword, but it was useless—the warrior's swords shattered the brute's sword and probably shattered his body too. All I heard was his sword shattering and a massive impact where the brute busted through a wall, dead. He emerged seconds later, his swords already sheathed. The fire that had seconds ago engulfed him was burning down. He passed the short man, who was trembling with fear. The warrior seemed to ignore him altogether, at least until the short man pulled out a sword. The short man's sword was shaking so badly you could see his poorly crafted blade wobble. Pulling out that weapon made the warrior stop dead; the short man was well behind the warrior, but neither of them moved, one out of fear and one out of patience. Finally after several moments of a silent, motionless standoff between the two, the short man made a slight move toward the warrior. The warrior quickly burst back into the red flames. He turned and threw a fireball that exploded the short man into flaming pieces that flew in every direction, after which he returned to normal and continued his approach.

The warrior walked toward me, but he didn't have that "I plan to set you on fire" look, so you'd think I'd be reassured—I wasn't. However, despite his scary nature, all he did once he reached me was offer his hand. I was still on the ground where I was so painfully tossed earlier. I took his hand, but I was so numb, and where I wasn't numb I hurt like hell, but I was still able to get to my feet for a second. I was standing for barely a few moments before my legs felt like they were broken and I collapsed. Luckily for me, the warrior was still there. He caught me before I fell and picked me up. It was kind of awkward, but I wasn't complaining. I knew I was safe. It's just strange. His armor felt smooth and cold to the touch. I couldn't feel any imperfections in the metal, and I could also feel the smooth carvings etched in the armor. Even the etchings were smooth and perfect. He carried me over toward the gate, where a familiar silhouette appeared in the gateway. The Janubian from across the sea whom I picked earlier, which got me into this situation, was standing there approaching us. I wasn't really sure what to make of my current situation. Guess the events of the past hour had exhausted my daily supply of fear because I was hardly afraid. He took from me the package that I took from him. The package was a sealed satchel made of hard, dark leather. The flap was sealed shut with a solid blue wax seal that looked unbroken. It was obvious that there was something roughly cylindrical within the satchel, but it was well obscured.

He felt the seal, checking to see that it was still sealed and that it hadn't been resealed. After he was assured he tucked the satchel into the robe he was wearing over his armor. It seemed almost planned, for as soon as the satchel was tucked away, a platoon of city garrison led by the ambitious captain Melic appeared through the far gates into yards. Etan Melic had made quite the name for himself as a captain, both because of his keen, diplomatic mind as well as his tactical aggressiveness. He has dissolved volatile situations peacefully and diplomatically whenever possible, but also he has slaughtered crime lords without mercy. Because of this he is well respected and well feared at the same time. He is often noted as a fair-minded man, and for this he is well liked in the more civil districts. Now why he would decide to wander into this district I will never know, but here he was.

"Well, they said that this district was being turned upside down by foreigners—guess they were right. I was surprised when I saw armed men running for their lives," Captain Melic said. He was followed by twenty-two heavily armored guards bearing the seal of the barony with the traditional blue and gold. The captain was speaking to the Janubian. The warrior stepped out of the obscure, dark corner still carrying me but seemingly not noticing that he was. The guards looked more than slightly confused as to why the warrior was holding me; however, no one said a thing. The captain glimpsed over with a sort of raised eyebrow at me, but his expression quickly changed as his eyes rose to the warrior's piercing gaze. It seemed liked he recognized the strange tattoo the warrior had on his face. I thought it was just a tattoo, but the captain seemed almost fearful of it, like it meant something bad. However, the captain didn't linger on it for too long to avoid conflict.

"What are you doing here? I can't say I have any sympathy for these deviants, and I'm sure they got what they deserve. However, I have to ask when some strangers start killing people even if they are street trash," the captain said, looking around at all the bodies that littered the bazaar. The warrior simply glared silently, letting the Janubian do all the talking, though he didn't seem subordinate to him.

"It was a situation that is now resolved. Suffice to say they came by some of my property without permission, and we required its reacquisition," he said without flinching and with a cocky smile. One of the guards approached the warrior and me, looking at me in particular. I didn't recognize this guard, but I had the feeling that he may have recognized me.

"Is this the one who 'acquired' your property? I hear she is good at that," he said, apparently approaching to apprehend me. However, as he neared, the warrior quickly shifted his gaze to the guard and tightened his grip on me. With a scowl he sent the guard back to the formation. The captain simply shook his head and continued his confrontation.

"Well, I'm pretty sure nobody is going to miss these low-life scums. However, I need to take you three in for further questions. It's just a formality but still."

"Oh, and why is that? It's not as though this attack was unprovoked or anything. Besides, the situation was resolved already. There is no reason for further alarm, Captain."

"Simply put, this wasn't some street mugging—this was a dust-town massacre. Besides, she has an outstanding warrant so her involvement in this requires further investigation. We also need to discern exactly what was stolen and whatnot. Like I said it's mostly a formality, but it is necessary," he explained without moving from formation.

"What will happen to her?" the Janubian asked, pointing back at me. The captain brought his hand to his mouth, obviously giving the question a great deal of thought.

He finally replied, "Well, she is still wanted for theft charges. Most are flimsy so she might spend a few years in jail but no more probably."

"Well, I'm sorry I can't allow you to take her. I have decided to take her along during my mission."

"That's not happening. She will not escape justice, not this time. If you pursue this matter you will be charged with harboring a fugitive. You have no authority to act on this, I will see her in a cell for as long as I can legally keep her there. She will not escape to continue her crimes elsewhere," he said, almost yelling. I had no idea I was so much of a pain. It feels good to know I was such a bother. It did seem like the two of them weren't going to let this just go like that. I did not, however, see the next part coming at all.

"I'm sorry, Captain. I do respect your sense of justice. However, I must recruit Kya into the Order of the Last Sentinel." The captain simply aired a look of disappointment, as he knew he had lost before anyone else did. It was obvious that nobody else had any idea what he was talking about. I know I didn't.

"Sentinels, huh? Now what is an outdated order like yours doing here?" asked the captain. All the guards were looking around, confused about what this "order" was and how they could avert justice by simply recruiting criminals.

"Sir, they can't just harbor criminals from justice. Who are they?" asked one of the guards to the captain.

"Their order has always shown an interest in the petty criminal. They consider it a rehabilitation, and most baronies accept their right to conscript criminals. However, no one has used it or even heard of any tale of your order in near a century. Why now?" asked the captain. The Janubian simply looked at the captain sideways and motioned for me and the warrior to come. The warrior slid his shoulders to readjust his swords as he began walking. As we passed through the battlefield littered with bodies, one of the men seemed to still be alive. The warrior just stepped over him, glaring down at the man as he walked by. The Janubian walked past the captain and his men, followed by the warrior still carrying me. The captain, obviously unpleased with the day's outcome, just stood still and allowed us to leave without incident. Not that I was worried. I am sure even then that the warrior was more than proficient enough to deal with them if the need had arisen. Shortly after we passed through the great gates of Kal'Hinrathos, I could finally feel my legs, though I didn't need to say anything. He seemed to know and put me down and continued on with me following. As we reached a distance I looked back from the top of one of the great hills overlooking the city and saw my familiar home as the sun set and the city with it. At this point I had ventured farther from its walls than I have ever been, and yet I did and didn't miss it. I was glad to belong to something other than myself. Of course I had no idea what I had become a part of, what was this Order of the Last Sentinel . . .

CHAPTER 2

THE GAUNTLET

Camping out in the forest didn't seem much different than being homeless in the city of Kal'Hinrathos' since both were equally as dangerous. In the forest there were all manner of creatures and beasts eager for a quick meal; in the city you need to look for murderers, slavers, and rapists all roaming the alleys at night. The Janubian whose name I later learned to be Halkiir Valkim said we were plenty safe here, as the creatures weren't quite aggressive enough to risk attacking us—that and the warrior never seemed to sleep. He just stood guard all night long. I asked often where we were heading, but Halkiir would only say it was for my initiation or something. He also said I would learn more about the order then as well. We traveled for about two weeks without any trouble until we reached a massive wind-shaped canyon of dark granite formed over what must have been millions of years, or some great cataclysm. Halkiir said there was a fortress built right into the stone at the end of the canyon that they've used as a stronghold for centuries. The canyon was nearly three miles in length, but the outer walls of Windrift Fortress was only a mile in. The walls were massive at sixty-five feet tall and over twenty feet thick of the seamless orangish red granite. The guards wore the similar red-and-white armor that Halkiir himself wore, implying a uniform of some kind. However, Halkiir's did seem far more complex as well as personalized compared to the garrison. I figured this meant he was a higher rank. From the way it looked, his armor was more like the traditional Janubian armor. It looked like he just tailored the same armor he likely wore in the deserts of Januus'Anub to the color pattern of the Sentinels. The walls and towers of the outer defense were crawling with soldiers wearing identical uniforms of their iconic red and white. Their armor definitely qualified as heavy, much heavier than that of Halkiir's. Their armor was some of the heaviest armor I've seen. Such armor is too expensive to issue to all the garrison of a fortress, especially one that's over two miles long with over seventy thousand defenders.

I found it odd that as we passed through the fortress the garrisoned troops and the other Sentinels did seem to wear a similar-themed armor and uniforms, but the warrior's armor was completely different in every way possible. I was enthralled by the subtle beauty of this fortress, the carved walls of the canyon and all the red-orange granite structures and towers. The fortified nature of the fortress was obvious as we must have passed through a dozen massive stone walls with gates of steel and stone. The keep, which was where we were heading, was a miracle of architecture. A twelve-floor keep carved at the end of the canyon, the entry hall alone was over eighty feet tall with overlooking towers and balconies with massive braziers, creating a well-lit environment even under hundreds of feet of solid granite. Halkiir was uncommonly quiet as we walked through the fortress, only exchanging greetings with his comrades as we passed. The warrior was stoic as usual with his expressionless gaze and didn't seem to know anyone at the fortress. For whatever reason, they obviously had great respect for him, but it seemed like they were looking more at the strange etching upon his armor as though they meant something.

Our destination was deep within the keep, down what felt like hundreds of stairs and through winding corridors of stone that all looked alike to me. Luckily, Halkiir knew the way. These halls had guards at almost every corner as well as patrols of four, which we encountered often as we moved deeper and deeper into the keep. After the longest spelunking adventure ever recorded, we finally reached a massive circular room with eleven great stone statues, each fifty feet tall, surrounding the room like stone Sentinels. There was a man in the middle of the room who wasn't wearing armor, but instead he wore a red-and-white cloak with a long, thin sword at his side. His sword seemed almost fragile because of how thin it was, but at this point I had no doubt that it was a deadly weapon in the right hands. Though this man did look old, I figured that just meant he was well experienced from many years of hard combat.

"Greetings, my old friend, I had not expected to see you back here for many months at least. How fares your quest?" said the old man to Halkiir as they clasped arms in a show of respect and friendship. It was quite obvious the way these two men greeted each other that they had some pretty intense history hidden behind their smiles.

"Ah, yes, I had not expected to be back. However, I have found a most-promising recruit I would like to add to my team as I continue upon my quest. After all I will need all the help I can get for this," Halkiir said without looking back at me or the warrior. The old man looked back to find the potential recruit. Naturally his eyes fell first on the warrior as he seemed the part more than I. However, as the old man's eyes fell upon him, the warrior crossed his arms and made a subtle nod in my direction. The old man then turned his head to me, but he did not seem at all disappointed in what he saw.

"I'm guessing this is she. Hmm, she looks quick and quiet. You have been nagging me for a scout for some time. I guess you found one yourself. Oh, she will me a valuable member I'm sure," the old man said.

"Oh yes, I'm counting on it, be sure," Halkiir said with a smile. The old man beckoned us forward, and so I followed him and Halkiir as we walked to the other side of the great chamber toward a set of massive stone doors on the other side. However, when I turned and looked the warrior was not with us. After looking about, I found him near where we had stopped before. He had gone to one of the statues to stand out of the way and had no intention of following us. I had fallen behind and had to hurry to catch up with Halkiir, who was talking in length to the old man about something or another. I only started paying attention when the warrior was brought up.

"And I see that he is here. So did you have it?" the old man asked.

"Indeed. He was most helpful in recovering them though there were far more than we had anticipated. I left the platoon there to recover the artifacts and bring them back as soon as they get them to their ships. I, however, brought something unexpected," he said, pulling out a brilliant diamond the size of a man's fist. This diamond was unique, as it was red in its center like it was a diamond on the outside and a ruby on the inside. I'm sure magic is at work here. I just have no idea what it is.

We all entered even deeper into the keep than before to begin a long and somewhat strange ritual as well as to take my oath. I must admit that I was unprepared to give my life into such a brotherhood. Now naturally, I cannot speak of the ritual itself, as it is a secret. All I can say is that it was something I did not expect—beautiful and magnificent. They didn't answer a lot of questions, but Halkiir said that now I was a Sentinel like him he would be glad to answer any questions once we went on our way—which was a shame, as I was getting used to a real bed and food.

We only stayed a few weeks. At camp the night after we left, I figured it was time for answers.

"Halkiir, what do Sentinels do exactly?" I asked. Halkiir was tending the fire while the warrior had disappeared, as was usual for him. Still have no clue where he goes or what he does this late. I figured with him gone Halkiir could answer questions, as I did not know if there were secrets he did not know.

"The Order of the Last Sentinel was created to defend against threats that normal people cannot imagine. We secure and protect from those who misuse great power to hurt the innocent and destabilize the fragile balance of peace. Usually we operate behind the scenes and out of sight. However, we have been dragged into the light once before. We've only made our presence known because of Danus Kellam, more commonly known as Dragonnaught, because he was corrupted by the Dragon Gauntlet," he explained. I know what you are about to ask, and yes, I asked too.

"The Dragon Gauntlet? What's a gauntlet?" Halkiir raised his right arm to reveal what I did actually already notice—his right gauntlet was different than the one he wore on his left arm. The gauntlet was metal, unlike the metal used in regular armor and left gauntlet. It was darker than the standard steel and had strange etchings that seemed to glow from within with a strange grayish light.

"The Gauntlet is a powerful magical artifact first created by the Triaegis Empire thousands of years ago before its unexplained disappearance. The Gauntlet is one of the only remaining clues to the untold magic they commanded. The Gauntlet allows the wearer to command a portion of the power imbued into it. All Gauntlets created for the Sentinels harness the powers of either wind or stone," he said, putting his arm down.

"How is this done?"

"I don't pretend to know how it is done. I do know that they are extremely difficult to make, both the physical shell as it is to imbue it. Only a few smiths are capable of this process. The Sentinels employ their own exclusively. All Sentinels have a Gauntlet. The ritual you went through determines which element your Gauntlet will be. See, Gauntlets are strange creations: they almost have a mind of their own. As such the Gauntlet must be made for you using the blood we took during your ritual. This makes your Gauntlet only useable to you. Also Gauntlets can be difficult to use, so using blood makes it easier for recruits to do so," he said, pulling out a leather satchel similar to the one I tried to steal originally from his bag. He broke the seal on it and pulled a beautiful Gauntlet from it. It was a blue-gray metal, and the etchings resembled wind as well as had a bluish glow to them. It was obvious that this Gauntlet was for me, as it was too small to fit either Halkiir or the warrior. He handed me the Gauntlet, which I took, somewhat fearful of its power. The Gauntlet was right-handed like his and looked similar in design; only the etchings and the colorations were different. He urged me to put it on to see how it fit. It was strange. When I first put it on, it seemed somewhat too big, but it adjusted itself. Also I could already feel a strange sensation through my arm. It felt like a cool breeze blowing across my skin. It was somewhat exciting to wear the Gauntlet, but aside from the sensation from the Gauntlet, I could not seem to control the power that was said to be within. He told me that control over the Gauntlet would take time. He himself took over two months to manipulate earth.

"Has anyone tried to combine two or more powers?" I asked, looking over my Gauntlet's beautiful design.

"The process of imbuing the Gauntlets will not allow for multiple magical essences. They conflict with each other. All attempts at such has always failed," he said, tending to the fire.

"Why not wear two Gauntlets and use them together?"

"No, never do that. Gauntlets are powerful magical objects that have what seems like their own personality. Because of this they conflict with one another, violently usually. Everyone who has attempted it has died," he said, looking very stern and serious.

"People have attempted it though. If it is deadly why would anyone try it?"

"Power, power or desperation," he said simply. He was quiet for a while, and as I was about to inquire further, he started again.

"You remember the stories of Aos and Al'Maquise?" Of course I had to say no. Stories weren't part of my street training. Luckily he was glad to tell it, so I'll just tell the story without those annoying little marks you have to put before a quote.

About six hundred years ago, when the knowledge of Gauntlet construction was still extremely young, the ancient Gauntlets left behind by the old empire dominated as rulers. There were three. The three were the most dominant in the Triaegis Empire held by the three kings of the empire. Each king was granted power from the most powerful creature of his kingdom, the Gryphon, the Phoenix, and the Dragon. The Gryphon was granted to King Kalydiin, who ruled the lands now known as Kaladiin'Aaiyyr and who was the greatest king of the Triaegis Empire. The Phoenix granted its power to Archon Naydiina, ruler of the eastern kingdom of Valjjain, which still bears the name. The Dragon granted his power and wisdom to Chaeyuun, ruler of the imperial province which is now the Empire of Chae to the west. After the collapse of the old empire, the magic that bound all other Gauntlets faded over the many millennia, except for the main three Gauntlets of the kings. All three were discovered though only two are publicly known. The Gryphon is still in the hands of the Kingdom of Adiin'Ayr but not many know of the Phoenix Gauntlet's discovery. However, for nearly a century the Dragon Gauntlet was used by the rulers of the west until something happened. We are not sure what happened, but the Gauntlet became corrupted by powerful and dark magic. Sensing the corruption, Nay'Kallium ceased his use of the Gauntlet and sealed it away. However, leading back up to six hundred years ago, a man guided by powerful instincts and visions discovered the corrupted Dragon Gauntlet and was in turn corrupted by its power. With the Gauntlet of the Dragon he was able to conquer much of the northern region of Inuskard then setting his eyes on conquering the rest of Kaladiin'Aaiyyr. The corrupted Dragon Gauntlet was more powerful than any other gauntlet, save for the other two ancient Gauntlets. Though the order possessing the Phoenix Gauntlet aided with troops and supplies, the Archon who wore the Gauntlet never took the field. As such it was King Jaedin who confronted the Dragon with the Gryphon.

This battle was held inside the greatest temple in the great city of Aaomysiir, capital of the Kingdom of Adiin'Ayr, where King Jaedin and Al'Maquise, formerly Danus Kellam, fought. The battle went on for nearly two days. The clashing of the Gauntlets unleashed such a frenzy of power that they leveled the temple. However, despite the Gryphon's power, the corrupted Dragon won out in the end, and King Jaedin fell in combat. The Sentinel commander of the time, Aos, entered the ruins of the temple. He knew his own gauntlet was not powerful enough and so he donned the king's Gauntlet as well and, with the combined power of the two, was able to defeat Al'Maquise. Only, moments after his victory, even after removing the Gauntlet, he died before anyone reached the field. The power of the two Gauntlets killed him with a magical conflict between them. The Gryphon Gauntlet was passed down to the next ruler, and the Dragonnaught Gauntlet was hidden and sealed away. This was the greatest victory for the Sentinels, and Aos is now widely considered a legendary hero of unmatched proportions. The two-Gauntlet technique has been attempted both before and after him. However, they never lasted more than a few minutes of intense combat, whereas Aos survived for nine hours. I guess the moral of this story is to never wear two Gauntlets despite the massive power it can give you. Apparently, Aos's Gauntlet was imbued by the powers from the Gryphon, and so all Sentinel Gauntlets are imbued by his Gauntlet. Though no one wears Aos's Gauntlet anymore, it remains within Windrift Fortress as the most holy of artifacts.

We talked for hours about the Sentinels and Gauntlets and all manner of other subjects, but he would never tell me what our mission was or anything about the warrior, not even his name. Eventually we both went to sleep. He said we had an early morning and a long day ahead of us the following day. I will admit sleeping in soft grass was a lot better than sleeping on the hard, cold stone back in the city. I could do without all the strange bugs though.

The following morning I awoke to the smell of breakfast, which smelled quite good actually. Before I could eat, Halkiir asked me to find the warrior. He suggested I search to the east of the camp. I started out. The east of the camp was leading into some heavily forested area. Now I have never seen so much green in my life, and I walked slowly as I was overwhelmed by color. There was so much here to see, whereas in the desert it is just sand and the occasional cactus. After a short time, I was totally lost. However, luck was, as usual, on my side, as I stumbled right where I needed to be. I wandered into a bandit camp, and though this would usually be considered a bad thing, luck is something I usually have when it comes to surviving. I was greeted by two dead bandits who had been cleaved into a multitude of small pieces and now resided in a soup of their blood and entrails. I entered the camp from the back end through a small, hidden path behind some hard tents. Why there were two dead people back here is beyond me, but whatever happened, they were really unlucky. As I walked between the tents toward what I hoped was the middle of the camp in an attempt to uncover what happened, the damage to the tents became more prevalent. The camp wasn't really that large, and I did find myself in the center of the camp, and what I found there was familiar. About twenty or thirty bodies all killed in gruesome ways, strewn about the campsite. As I watched, utterly mortified at this, I could hear sounds approaching from the other end of the campsite. I obviously took to hiding, so I returned to where I entered. From this vantage point I could see into the courtyard while remaining unseen. What I saw next was unexpected, and a tad creepy. The warrior entered the camp dragging some dead guy by the ankle. He reached the center of the courtyard and dropped the body and looked directly at me with his emotionless gaze. However, he did not say anything or gesture at me. He just left me in hiding. Shortly after he dragged the body into the camp, another warrior arrived from the same direction that he had come from. The new warrior was the most gorgeous woman I've ever seen, and I don't mind saying so. She had an air of elegance, but was also clearly a solider, or a knight, I guess. She had platinum-white hair like the warrior. Her armor was almost as complicated as the warrior's, though not with the maddening angles. Her armor was clean, really clean, and shiny too. Her armor consisted of numerous individual plates covering main areas of the body, augmented by the shiniest chain mail I have ever seen. Unlike the warrior's armor, which seems almost seamless, her armor was a multitude of smaller pieces attached by a set of chain mail that I have never seen before.

She and the warrior obviously knew each other by the way they were acting around each other. Well, that and she was just as emotionless as him, cold yet beautiful. She wore a long spear, a design unlike any normal spear. The spear was unusually ornate and well designed for complex situations. The spear had a long, narrow head that was both sharp enough and narrow enough to be armor piercing. At the bottom of the head were two symmetrical blades for sweeping attacks. Below even that were two long spikes about six inches out of the shaft. These spikes must have been for dismounting cavalry or impaling ground infantry on sweeps. This spear appeared to be very brutal and designed for war, not guard duty. The spear had groves, slits, and various designs for both visual and combat purposes. Kal'Hinrathos is notable for spears, so I have seen a great many types, but never one like this or one even close. Of course her armor was by far too thick to assess how strong she was, though she must be able to use that massive spear. I did remain in hiding, but I'm not really sure why. It was obvious that both of them knew I was there. After several minutes of watching from a distance, I finally decided to come out of hiding. I was reasonably sure that they already knew I was there by then anyway. When I reached the central courtyard, neither of them seemed surprised to see me, further proving my point.

"Kya, this is Kara," said the warrior in his usual emotionless tone.

"Hello, Kara. It's nice to meet you. Any friend of . . . uh . . . him is a friend of mine," I said, just realizing that I still have no idea what his name is.

"You must be Halkiir's newest Sentinel. He usually has a good eye for ability. He also knows that powerful people can show up in the most unlikely of places," she said, looking down at me. Now before you get the wrong idea, she was looking down at me because she was tall, not because she thought I was inferior. You see, that would require her to actually *feel* something first. Of course I'm not short either; she's just tall, like five foot ten or eleven. Come to think of it, Halkiir is five foot ten; of course the warrior is like six six or seven, giant as he is. Now back on point. I have no idea how she knew where I was from, as she said "unlikely of places," which meant she knew I was from the streets. After all, I had changed into the traditional red and white clothing of the Sentinel with limited to no armor properties, and I also bathed. I guess the warrior must have told her. Speaking of uniforms, she wore a small triangular cape that stretched to about her midback. It was black with a silver lining. It appeared to be the same color scheme as the warrior's armor, suggesting some kind of familiarity between the two of them. However, her armor was unlike his in both design and color. Hers was black, augmented by shiny purple designs painted on them. The chain mail she wore was white steel and was platinum colored with the slightest golden tint and just as shiny. Based on the shiny nature of her armor, I'd say it was either a dress uniform or she was way too wealthy to even go into. I was wrong on both accounts . . .

At the time I was a bit more worried about why the warrior was dragging a body by the leg into a camp of dead people. The wounds on the people were consistent with the warrior's dual-wielded long swords. By the looks of the dead, they were wilderness folk for sure, probably bandits, so I wasn't sorry to see them dead.

"Uh, why did you kill a camp full of people for?" I asked, looking around.

"They were bandits intent on assaulting a nearby village. I was sent to prevent this from happing and requested the aid of an old friend," Kara said in an all-too-familiar emotionless tone. I swear if these two aren't related, they should be. Now I'm not going to go into how massively overkill it was to bring these two to a fight with a bunch of bandits but hey, guess they'll take any excuse to see each other. Everything soon became clear moments after our talk. Dozens of bandits on horseback rode up to the camp, and I knew that someone was going to die, but just not who they thought. Of course I figured that the warrior would just cut them down without a thought. Not exactly what happened though, and what did, surprised everyone. They apparently were more than your garden-variety bandit thugs, as they had hedge wizards with them. Now from what I understand about magical lore, Gauntlets are not required for magical use. However, the Gauntlet focuses the magic user's power, allowing for more powerful magic that would consume those without a Gauntlet. Still, not all mages are equal. Even with the same Gauntlet type, one mage may be more powerful than another. It simply makes that mage more powerful. However, Gauntlets are extremely—and let me emphasize *extremely*—hard to make; so it was much to our surprise when their merry gaggle of bad guys showed up with not one but three Gauntlets in their possession. To make things worse, the man riding to the right of the warlord or whatever was wearing purple robes with white trimming. This was the traditional robes of the Collegium, the magical college in Aaomysiir. The Aaomysiir Collegium is sanctum for the Magus Arcana or a mage's collective. The Collegium has its own unique Gauntlets given to members of the Magus Arcana upon graduating.

His Gauntlet was clearly visible and very ornately designed, much more so than our Sentinel Gauntlets. He was my main worry, as he was a trained mage. The other two, however, I couldn't recognize their Gauntlets. They seemed far less ornate; they looked very basic in construction. They may not have been the best looking, but they were still Gauntlets and therefor dangerous weapons. Now I can see that Kara had a Gauntlet as well, but I'm not sure where she got hers from.

"You killed all my obviously overpaid associates. Well, guess I should thank you. You just saved me a lot of gold. However, I will have to find and hire more useless thugs for my plan. I cannot allow you to continue to interfere with my . . . what's with the midget Sentinel?" he asked, looking at me with his head cocked slightly to the right. Both Kara and the warrior looked back at me with the same empty look they always seem to have. However, this time it was a little different. It was almost as if they were wondering why I was here too. How stupid I felt now when all I could muster up was a stupid, awkward smile and some awkward grunt. After the awkward moment had passed, Kara and the warrior shifted their collective gazes back to the bandits. Apparently, the bandits got tired of waiting around, and one of the lesser mages used his Gauntlet to attack Kara. Luckily, Kara was really fast and countered with a blast of her own. They were both fireballs, but the mage's was a simple yellow flame, and hers was a brilliant blue flame. It was like their Gauntlets were fighting each other, and I'm certain that hers would have won if not for the interference. The Collegium mage stepped in, blindsiding her from the right with a magical bolt, sending her to the ground. She was unharmed by the blast, but still. The hedge mage who attacked first tried again, but the warrior stepped in the way and caught the blast in a blaze of bright red fire.

The second hedge mage tried to assist his friend with a similar blast of fire. However, it was completely useless. The warrior simply moved his left hand within which he had caught the first blast to catch the second blast as well holding both attacks back with a single Gauntlet. The two idiots were trying to maintain their attacks, but it was taking a toll, and it was clear they couldn't keep it up much longer. So seeing the trouble they were having, the Collegium mage tried his side-swipe trick again, and was he surprised at what came next. The warrior deflected the blast with his right hand, sending the blast flying right back at the mage who had to dodge, nearly falling off his horse in the process.

"Only a powerful Gauntlet could have redirected that blast, and your Gauntlet is left-handed?" The blasts from the other two mages dissipated, and they collapsed on the ground. The crimson fire around his left arm slowly burned into nothing as he turned to face the last remaining mage. The warrior turned around and went to Kara's side to check on her. Neither of them said anything, but they had some kind of unspoken communication. The warrior stood up, helping Kara up as well. She appeared okay, but what was truly remarkable was that she kept her cold, emotionless expression. The warrior looked back at me, and his eyes had turned that fiery red, which was my cue to make myself scarce. He began to engulf himself in fire, only even more fiercely red than the last time. As I watched, his eyes turned to a red, fiery color to match the flames he was creating. Kara had drawn her unusual spear and was ready to combat mounted opponents. Her spear was beautiful, but its beauty was a mask for its devastating killing ability. Now it would appear that the bandits had all the advantages; they had the numbers, the weapons, and they were on horseback. The bandits had fifteen mounted members, two of which were the hedge mages and the Collegium mage. The soldiers were armed like crazy with spears, swords, and a wicked-looking flanged mace. When the attack began it started so quickly that I didn't even realize what was happening at first. The first horseman to charge was right at Kara. That was a particularly bad idea, for the horseman didn't last very long at all. Poor horse. The horseman charged at her, but she held her ground. She buried her shoulder plate into the neck of the horse, probably killing the poor creature but definitely knocking it and the rider to the ground. A quick thrust of her spear tip easily dispatched him permanently from existence. She sidestepped just in time to avoid being speared through. She was able to react quickly using the right-side spike to dismount him by stabbing him in the chest, knocking him to the ground. She quickly slit his throat with the blade on her spear.

I have never seen a warrior move so quickly with such a massive weapon. She used this powerful weapon with such grace and perfection. She almost effortlessly manipulated her spear. Her perfection and proficiency in battle was extremely impressive. It made the bandits think twice before they tried to attack again. Of course at the same time, the warrior was being his usual calm and calculating self. He didn't even pull his weapon and instead approached the bandit leader. The leader's bodyguards, or whatever they were, weren't too happy about it. Two mounted goons with better weapons and armor than the rest charged at the warrior clumsily. The bandit from the left was first to get at the warrior, but the warrior simply dodged out of the way with a single, quick move, no gesture wasted. Of course after he missed he naturally turned to try again. However, the second bandit arrived first with a long spear, trying the same thing. The warrior shifted to the right, grabbing the spear and pulling the rider to the ground. The warrior then used the sharp edge of the spear tip to slice open the grounded bandit. I could see the blood splatter up but not where he was sliced. The warrior turned toward the fast-returning first rider who was armed with a sword and small buckler. The rider was already leaning partially left trying to get a good swipe at the warrior when he noticed the spear he had. The warrior didn't even bother waiting for him to get close; instead he just threw it. The throw was perfect, going straight through his neck about six inches. This sent him flying off his horse, where I'm sure he died shortly after. The mage was next to try and kill the warrior, this time with a magical bolt of some kind. He jerked gracefully to the right as the bolt flew right past him. He looked up at the mage. One of the other mages figured he'd take advantage of the distraction to get a shot off; he was in error. He fired a very typical fireball, but the warrior responded with something a bit more original.

The warrior, without looking, sent a massive boulder flying right at him, taking the fireball with it. The mage's eyes got bigger than a fruit when he saw it coming, but he was too slow to avoid it. It hit him, making a very distinctive crunch. The horse was okay, but the boulder took the mage about ten feet away, crashing into some trees. He never took his eyes off the Collegium mage. Kara took out one of the other mages, and the warrior took care of the other with a boulder, leaving only the Collegium mage and the bandit leader. Kara carved her way through most of the bandits, save the ones killed by the warrior and the two left. Kara came to the warrior, probably to provide backup, if needed. The remaining mage was at the right hand of the bandit leader, where he hadn't moved since they first arrived, despite the annihilation of all the others. The mage dismounted and approached the warrior with his staff and Gauntlet glowing with energy. Seeing this, Kara moved out of the way, knowing what was coming next. The mage stopped about fifteen feet in front of the warrior. They both stood so still, watching each other for the longest time. The mage was first to act, which I have come to expect—the warrior will never act first. The mage sent a series of attacks at the warrior, using both his Gauntlet and his staff, one after another. He wielded his staff left-handed with his Gauntlet right-handed, firing an endless series of attacks at the warrior. The warrior disappeared behind smoke and debris tossed up by the attacks. It was scary seeing him disappear into smoky oblivion, but I had faith he was all right. My faith was rewarded when I saw him protected behind a wall of bright red flame that was absorbing his attacks. He was only visible after the mage stopped his attacks. The mage was most surprised that his attacks were utterly futile.

The next move was neither something I expected nor I can truly explain it. The mage started a new, sustained attack that looked powerful. His attack was a bluish magical flame that consumed the warrior. However, the warrior struck back with a blinding attack of pure white energy. His right Gauntlet was thrust forward, projecting the energy forward. What I could not understand was there was a silhouette standing with him, and he was mimicking its movements or perhaps it's his. The silhouette looked like a woman with the same Gauntlet but not the armor. She appeared to be floating next to him, assisting him. She was formed from the pure light or perhaps emitting it. The light took only a second to engulf the mage and his attack, though it felt more like an eternity. After the light had faded, the mage was nowhere to be found; only his Gauntlet remained sitting on the ground while the rest was simply gone. The bandit leader leaned forward with his jaw open in surprise. The bandit leader, being the only one left, quickly escaped into the distance. Kara and the warrior were both content to allow him to go without a word. I decided it was about time for me to come on out since the danger had just ran off scared. I joined Kara and the warrior when they were coming back into the camp. When I met up with them, Kara put her non-Gauntleted right hand tight on my head. I guess it was just more proof of how short I was compared to her. I wasn't sure whether to shake her hand off or just leave it be. I figured just to leave it. After all, her hand was big enough to cover my head in her plate and chain-mail gauntlet. Please note that I am not talking about her magical Gauntlet, just a regular steel glove. For future reference, when I am talking about the magical ones, I will spell them with a capital *G* since it's something called a proper noun or something of the sort.

Halkiir finally decided to come looking for me after I have been gone for a long time. The warrior walked to greet him, and Kara followed close behind, taking her hand off my head. It was okay. I had already forgotten that it was there. Halkiir was looking around at all the bodies with the same reaction that I had. Kara turned and looked back at me, and I swear I saw a faint smile—good to see some emotion for a change.

"Kya, you getting into trouble?" he asked, looking around at all the bodies. I simply shrugged, having nothing to say. He looked over at Kara with a confused look. I was expecting Halkiir to know her—why not, he knows everyone else. I was surprised to see that he didn't know her. I would never have expected the warrior to be such a mystery to everyone, except Kara perhaps. I got the feeling from Kara's cold nature and her obvious loyalty to the warrior that she wasn't going to say anything about him. Of course that is if she actually knows anything about him. By Halkiir's look, he couldn't figure out to what order she belonged to, making her almost as big a mystery as him. At least she had a name though.

"Uh, Kya, who's your friend? I don't think we've met," asked Halkiir, looking over at Kara.

"Her name is Kara. She's a friend of mine actually," said the warrior, stepping out of the shadows behind Kara and putting his hand on her shoulder. Kara turned to look at him with that same faint smile I saw earlier.

"I see. Well, nice to meet you, Kara. It's nice to meet friends of, well, our friend. Have you and he been friends for a long time?" he asked. She was quiet for a long time, looking over at the warrior. He nodded slightly as if giving some kind of okay to talk about his past.

"Yes, I've known him for a very long time. He saved my life once. I had nothing left, so I decided to go with him. I had nowhere else to go."

"Well, it seems like you are a very capable knight. Why not join us? I'm sure our friend will be glad to have you along," said Halkiir.

"I'd like that. It's good to be useful. Besides, if you've recruited my friend, then this mission of yours must be important, you'll need all the help you can get," she said.

"We're glad to have you, Kara. We are heading to Kan'Varil and eventually Aaomysiir," said Halkiir.

"I came from Kan'Varil. They are having problems along the west road to Aaomysiir. The Fifth Legion was dispatched as well as a contingent of Gryphon Knights. I was there trying to assist when I was sent to take care of these bandits who were preying on this area in the absence of the legion. I was intending to head back to report my success," Kara explained.

"Yes, I fear the attack on Kan'Varil is closely related to our mission," Halkiir said, brushing his hand through his beard. Halkiir wandered off, obviously deep in thought, when he saw the Gauntlet from the mage still sitting where it fell. Halkiir was understandably both confused and curious about why a precious Gauntlet like this was just sitting on the ground without a body. He picked up the Gauntlet, which looked intact except that it no longer had its inner light. He studied it intently as though he had never even heard of a Gauntlet losing its light like this.

"This Gauntlet originated from the Collegium. What happened to it?" asked Halkiir as he turned and headed back to our group. Everyone was quiet for a long time. The warrior obviously didn't care to explain what happened since he said nothing either. He actually turned and walked away into the forest.

Kara was the first to speak. "Magica Vyrnum Xakila," she said. Now if this is confusing, don't worry—I was the same way. I had no clue what she was talking about, but apparently Halkiir did because his expression was something between fear and shock; I couldn't tell if he was more shocked or afraid. Figures I had to ask what it was that she was talking about. He simply looked at me, trying to figure out how to explain it. Kara obviously noticed that the warrior had disappeared and went to look for him. Here it took only a few moments for her to disappear completely out of sight in the trees behind the camp.

"Its dark magic, very dark magic," he said. "It's believed to be magic that was responsible for the destruction of the Triaegis Empire. The Vyrnum means it is magic that originated from the essence of the void, which, according to ancient lore, captured the first spark of magic. I have never heard of anyone who was able to control Vyrnum, as it, by nature, corrupts everything."

"How does it do whatever it is that it did?" I asked.

"Magica Arancnia requires energies from our own essence in order to create the spells we use. This, however, takes quite a toll on the body and soul, making it impossible to maintain spells indefinably. There are ways to extend or supplement that supply of energy so they can maintain their spells through long engagements of course. Certain herbs and poultices have been known to increase the mage's mana, but only a little. Drawing mana from other mages' own spells is extremely effective for Spell Breakers but is a difficult discipline to learn. Among the more unacceptable forms is blood magic, drawing mana from the blood of others. However, the void provides a virtually inexhaustible source of energy for the mage to use. They can draw great amounts of energy from the void, but the more they draw, the more dangerous it is due to the corruptive nature of the Vyrnum."

"Why has no one ever tried to use this type of magic before?"

"It's too dangerous. The Vyrnum draws all life out of our world. In order to use it, it must be controlled so as to only draw out small amounts. Despite much attempts, this kind of control is impossible."

"Then what is the spell that the warrior used?"

"According to this, Kara, he used a spell that drew the magical essence out of this Gauntlet and its wearer, much like the essence of the void drew in the spark of magic. At least this is what It seems. This level of magic is not supposed to exist. Not even the Triaegis Empire unlocked the secrets of Vyrnum. They tried for many centuries, but it was eventually banned after an experiment caused an explosion that sank an entire island off the coast. The Vyrnum was believed to have caused the great cataclysmic event that crumbled the old empire and changed the world. The Vyrnum is not just a power of destruction but of creation as well . . ."

CHAPTER 3

SIEGE

The smoke from the burning villages could be seen for miles. The castle at Kan'Varil, while still under siege, had held the marauders from encroaching further into the kingdom. The king's armies were on the march but were spread across the kingdom, dealing with attacks from all over. Most of these attacks are dealt with by this time, but these soldiers were spread too far and wide to be recalled for a march to Kan'Varil's aid. The attack on Kan'Varil happened only after the king had sent legions to deal with the growing number of attacks across the kingdom, so only a few were left during the assaults on Kan'Varil. From what Kara had said, Kan'Varil would have to stand alone. Halkiir and I started off along the Southern Road toward Kan'Varil from Windrift, along the southern border near Kal'Hinrathos. He said that the warrior and his friend would catch up at some point, as it was common for him to leave their party and scout ahead. It took us over a week of boring and uneventful walking from Windrift to reach this point. As we walked, we reached what looked like a garrison on the road, turning travelers away from the danger on the roads. The captain looked like he was a knight, whereas the others were merely soldiers. The Knight Captain put his hand up for us to stop as he walked toward us, obviously not afraid or suspicious of our arrival.

"Hail there, travelers, the road ahead is not fit for travel," he said from behind a full metal helmet. His voice kind of echoed from within. His armor bore the markings of a knight of the Royal Army. I can't figure out why a knight would be assigned to road duty and not some nameless footman.

"I am Knight Sentinel Halkiir from Windrift. This is Knight Sentinel Kya. We are here to assist at the Siege at Kan'Varil." The solider looked back to where the smoke clouds were coming from.

"Yes, some of your fellows passed this way not too long ago, some Kinterson guy and about twelve others," the knight said, pointing down the road with his thumb. Halkiir simply nodded and motioned for us to move on. The knight let us pass with no trouble and returned to his encampment beside the road. There were barely a dozen men with the knight, none of which were knights, just soldiers. By his lack of support, I can figure he wasn't expecting a fight this far from the battlefield.

"Strange," Halkiir said completely without context as we left earshot of the encampment. Of course I asked him what was so strange.

He replied, "That knight was from the Royal Army. I can't figure why he is guarding the road instead of sending aid to the fortress. Also he said Kinterson was here with a detachment. I have no idea why the Prelate would send him."

"Who is this Kinterson? Is he dangerous?" I ask, obviously.

"Yes, very. Kinterson is the Knight Captain of a particularly violent and successful detachment. He has hunted down and killed many demons and dark creatures throughout the years without mercy. Kinterson is the guy you send when you no longer value discretion." After that, Halkiir was strangely mute the rest of the trip. His discovery of Kinterson's involvement bothered him greatly. I got the feeling that he knew Kinterson and had some unforgotten memory about him in his past.

The next part I can remember very clearly; it's not something easily forgotten. We had been traveling much of the day away and were but a few hours away from making camp somewhere off the road, as we usually did. The sun was sinking low in the eastern sea, which for the first time in my life was out of sight behind mountains and hills. As we lost sight of the sun behind the low canyon walls that the road winded through, we were ambushed by what had to be the lamest ambush I have ever seen. The first three guys just walked along the road toward us. I looked back; Halkiir didn't. To block our exit, a couple other guys arrived behind us. However, at this point we were already two or three miles into the canyon, so they couldn't just follow us. Instead they jumped down from the walls. The first two made it quite nicely, but the third one tripped and fell to his death. He landed on his neck at the base of the canyon, making a very eerie crack. The two guys at our backs tried to help the guy, but he was clearly dead.

Halkiir pulled his long scimitar and his heavy-looking round shield off his back in preparation for holding off the three guys in the front. That left the two guys in the back to me. Now keep in mind I am a thief, not a murderer. I've never killed anyone before. Halkiir gave me two short swords for weapons, probably because of my fascination with the warrior's fighting style. He said it was to take advantage of my natural agility. I guess part of that must have been true. The bandits, obviously aware they were going to get nothing from us, decided to take action instead. They grunted and charged. All I saw was a guy flying into a wall to Halkiir's left, Halkiir having shield bashed the guy half to death. Then I had problems of my own to worry about. The two guys who didn't fall to their deaths in the back came after me.

My thief instincts were yelling, "Climb the walls! Escape, you fool!" Yet I stayed. I knew I had to keep them from getting at Halkiir's back. He trusted me to watch his back. The first guy who underestimated me struck low. My reflexes jumped me almost unconsciously from harm and he missed striking naught but dirt where I used to be standing. While the first guy fumbled, looking for me like an idiot, the second guy took his turn. I was against the canyon wall when he struck and swung an attack for my head. I ducked and rolled from harm as his sword found naught but stone. While still on one knee behind the guy, something told me to go for the legs. So I buried my blade in his right leg just below the knee. He screamed as I pulled my blade out and warm crimson blood splattered out on my hands and face. I was stunned from all the blood and his screams. He fell to his knee, dropping his sword. I could hear the first guy coming at me, obviously angry I just stabbed his friend. He swung an overhand swing right at me. It was clumsy and easily dodged. However, the result of me dodging was far more extreme than I could have known. His swing may have missed its target but still it found flesh, which it tore asunder. His blade cut right into his partner, slicing through his shoulder and removing his entire right arm. He screamed again even louder than the first. His screams were short-lived, as he fell over and passed out.

The blood was everywhere, flowing and squirting all about. The first man, having seen what he did, was taken aback by his accidental strike, enough for me to act. I spun around and sliced the back of his right knee (because that worked so well the last time) with my right blade. He fell to the ground, where I sunk my left blade all the way to the cross guard in his ear. For a moment there I could feel his heartbeat as he died. I swear, pulling the blade out was harder than putting it in. By time the fight was over, Halkiir had already been finished and was waiting for me to kill my enemy. He knew it was my first kill, and he knew I had to go through it, like some dark initiation. I just sat there among the dead; I'm not ashamed to admit it. There is something unnatural about taking the life of another human, but we do what we must.

"Does it get easier?" I asked as Halkiir as he helped me up.

"Eventually, you can fool yourself into believing that it does."

Later at camp we spent half the night cleaning the blood off our clothes and weapons, as well as searching through what we acquired from the dead bandits. He took my mind off the killing by having me appraise the valuable belongings of the dead. He said since we operated so far from Windrift and the order, sometimes we had to find more creative ways to earn living money. I spent the night doing that since I couldn't sleep. By morning I was feeling better. I told myself that if I hadn't killed him, he would have killed me and tried to kill Halkiir. I guess that made me feel better. Besides, it's not like he was any kind of innocent himself.

Halkiir said we would be in sight of Kan'Varil by midday, but it wasn't quite what I expected. By midday, as he predicted, we had reached an overlook from which we could see the burning villages around the fortress and the siege engines trying to breach its walls. However, Kan'Varil's walls were strong, too strong to be taken down by the small siege machines that they brought. At the overlook we also saw the other detachment of Sentinels lead by Kinterson. They all wore identical heavy armor with an assortment of weapons, but Kinterson wore something different. His armor has a lot more red in it than the standard issue, making him stand out a bit. It was clear that he noticed us because he was waiting for us when we came down the hill into the burnt village of Hale. The discussion that followed was unpleasant to say the least. Kinterson was waiting in one of the mostly intact buildings when we arrived. He kind of ambushed us in the town square.

"Ahh, Halkiir, don't you have some menial task to perform elsewhere? If I remember correctly, war is my area?" Kinterson said as he appeared from within a half-burned building. The tension in the air was like black, suffocating smoke—so thick it was nearly deadly.

"Kinterson, so what made the Prelate let the hound off his leash?" Halkiir remarked, obviously unimpressed by Kinterson's bravado.

"The Prelate knew that the siege at Kan'Varil needs more aid than an old man and a little girl can offer. The two of them approached, and it looked like they were going to come to blows with each other. Yet when they reached each other they just laughed and greeted each other as friends. Whatever bad blood there was between them was completely feigned. Kinterson's men must have been aware of their friendship, as they were not surprised by it.

"I was surprised to hear you were dispatched to deal with the situation at Kan'Varil," Halkiir said. Kinterson smiled slightly and walked back up the wooden stairs into the ruined building, turning at the door.

"War is what I know, Halkiir, and there is more to this than just bandits and marauders." Kinterson turned back into the door and disappeared into the building. He was subsequently followed by the rest of his men and eventually Halkiir and myself. The inside of the building was actually nicer than the outside suggested. Apparently Kinterson and his men had already cleared out the inside, as it was empty save for a large, round table in the center of the main floor. Kinterson and a few other Sentinels were gathered around the table. On the table was a map of the area indicating military forces at and around Kan'Varil. From what I can understand, there were more enemy forces in the area then our forces. The map was full of red marks and lines. According to the map, the royal military forces were on the very edge of the map and nowhere near Kan'Varil. There was only a small green arrow near the outskirts of the fortress.

"We can't expect that the king's forces will arrive in time to save Kan'Varil. That leaves the situation up to us and whatever forces we can gather," Kinterson said as he pointed down his map. I'm not sure where he got his map, but it was no ordinary cloth map. On his map the small pieces that represented forces actually moved, allowing him to monitor troop movements in real time. I'm not sure what kind of magic was at work, but it was obviously common, as no one was surprised by it. What I gathered from the map was Kinterson's forces were gathered in three camps around Kan'Varil. I'm not sure how many members of the Sentinels he had but apparently quite a few, all indicated in blue. I've been to Windrift Fortress, and it had a sizable garrison, but I was told they were not used for mobile operations. The king's forces were a long way away in the north, near Aaomysiir. According to his map, they were remaining near the capital. Now there was a small detachment of allied soldiers indicated by a green arrow, but they appeared to be withdrawing from the fortress.

"Any reports about the garrison of Kan'Varil and how they are doing?" Halkiir asked.

"From what I know so far they are holding the outer walls and have a full garrison. Luckily, Kan'Varil's soldiers are superior to the marauders. However, they can't hold out forever," Kinterson said. They were explaining some likely important but utterly boring strategies and only ended when we heard a strange and ominous squealing. The squealing was replaced by an even worse sound, an explosion. A nearby building exploded into a fireball, which was visible through a window. The force and heat could be felt through the walls, as everything shook violently. Before we could even question what happened, another squeal was heard, followed by another massive explosion—only closer. The shock we were in was immediately replaced by panic.

"Move!" Kinterson and Halkiir yelled simultaneously. We all rushed out the door. I thoughtfully grabbed the map off the table. It might have just been my thief nature to take it, but still. We escaped the building just in time, as the third impact was a direct hit, destroying the building. The explosion sent me flying several feet away with so much force I couldn't breathe for several seconds after. As I lay gasping for air on the ground, someone grabbed my leg and started pulling me away. Luckily it was a grassy field or my head would have suffered. Of course I'm glad they did, as not a minute after I was dragged away, the area where I had been lying erupted into a fireball. I clasped my arms over my face to avoid being blinded by the light and heat. When the heat stopped, I moved my arms to see two sets of feet and legs. They were the telltale armor of the warrior and Kara. One moment it was their legs, and then it was their backs I saw as they stood firm. It was all rather interesting to see the world passing by upside down, and confusing when I was released and able to stand up finally. At this point I saw that it was Kinterson who had grabbed me. I saw the next shot falling from the sky with that same scream, only this time it hit an invisible wall and bounced off, flying back toward the hills. It impacted and exploded a safe distance away from the village. Two more shots were fired and had the same effect, bouncing and exploding safely away from us and them.

"What is going on, mages?" I asked, having finally gotten the ringing out of my ears.

"Shh, cannons," someone replied. I was too busy focusing on the battle in front. Magic surrounded both the warrior and Kara in a similar way. The magical shroud around Kara was bluish white as the shroud around the warrior was a fiery red. They spoke an enchantment together, words unlike that I have heard. At the end a burst of magic shot forward and water, and fire were drawn forth. Fire swept from the warrior's side as water swept forward from Kara's side. The fire and water thrust into the ground with great force, sending grass and dirt flying about. Moments later a solider of clay climbed out of the ground, followed by more of his kind. They were perfect copies of each other. They were like an army of statues called forth to fight. The cannon's steel projectile descended from the sky again as it had before. This time the first of the clay men caught the cannon ball and dropped it onto the ground as they marched. Two dozen of them marched in formation. They disappeared over the hill, presumably to the enemy position; their disappearance was quickly followed by screams and war cries alike. The clash of steel lasted but minutes before the men of clay reappeared on the top of the hill, returning to the warrior and Kara. They returned to them severely shy and kneeled. Having completed their mission, they returned to the earth where they came. Halkiir got up and approached them, followed closely by Kinterson and his men. I eventually followed myself.

"What are you doing here, Xaddjyk, and why would you bring Vengeance with you?" Kinterson said as he approached them.

"All this time has she served, all this time has she been loyal," Xaddjyk replied, turning to face Kinterson. As notice to the readers, from now on I will be referring to the warrior as Xaddjyk, pronounced *zadh-ickt*. Xaddjyk's expression was hidden behind a black helmet, which had the same intricate and maddening design as the rest of his armor. Kara scouted around using her spear like a walking staff as she usually did. I'm not sure why Kinterson called her Vengeance, but she didn't seem to mind at all. She followed the path the clay soldiers took over the hills. As Xaddjyk and Kinterson talked about something, she disappeared completely over the hill.

"You two go watch her," Kinterson said, pointing over the hill while looking over at two Sentinels. The two Sentinels nodded and ran after her. Xaddjyk removed his helmet, revealing his expressionless face. He looked up toward the hill and waited. I'm not sure what he was waiting for, but it became clear soon after. I walked next to Xaddjyk, trying to figure out what he was looking for. The two Sentinels came limping over the hill, leaning on each other. It was obvious even at a distance that they were not seriously injured, just beaten silly.

Xaddjyk shook his head, walking away. He said, "Saw that coming." Kara appeared after them at the top of the hill with a large bag in her left hand as she continued to walk with her spear walking staff. The bag in her hand looked like it was full of dirt or sand, definitely something powdery, as the bag changed shape as she walked. She was in absolutely no hurry to reach us, and Xaddjyk was in no hurry for her to. She threw the bag to Kinterson, expecting him to know what it was. He pulled a handful of black sand from within the bag, allowing it to flow from his fingers back into the bag.

"What is this?" Kinterson asked. He handed the bag to Xaddjyk, who did a similar examination of the powder. It is impossible to know what he was thinking because of his amazing gambler's face.

"Cannons, collect the remainder of the black powder and destroy the cannons," Xaddjyk said to Kara, who quickly headed back to the hill. Kinterson was obviously confused; I'm guessing that like me, he never saw such an invention before. Now if you are like me, you are now wondering if Kinterson didn't know what a cannon was. The answer, I honestly haven't a clue, but that is seriously bugging me too. Xaddjyk was in quite a hurry to ensure this technology didn't fall into use by the brigands again. These "cannons" appeared less powerful than the power wielded by mages but far easier to use. Mages are actually fairly rare in modern society. History tells us that in the Triaegis Empire the gift of magic was extremely common. However, this gift has waned over the thousands of years, and Gauntlets are extremely hard to make and do require the gift. I can understand why any army would want a weapon that shoots fire from a distance without magic at all. I can also understand why Xaddjyk would want it destroyed before someone else got a hold of it. A few minutes after Kara disappeared over the hill, she returned, followed by a massive explosion.

"Are these Aegis cannons, Xaddjyk?" Halkiir asked, sounding calm despite everything. Xaddjyk remained silent until Kara approached, throwing him a large black ball a little smaller than a cantaloupe.

He looked at it carefully for several seconds before saying, "No, these cannons are extremely primitive. We no longer fire spherical projectiles." He tossed the cannonball just as emotionless as always.

"If they have access to cannons, primitive or not, the old walls of Kan'Varil will probably not hold for long," Kara said. Luckily Kan'Varil was just over the hill from us to the west. From the top of the hill, we could see the valley where the castle stood under siege. Kan'Varil stood in the center of a low plain about six miles from the hill where we were standing. The road leading to Kan'Varil was littered with burning buildings from the old villages that surrounded the castle. The farms that once supplied food to Kan'Varil that litter the plains were set ablaze by the marauders during their push against the walls. From what we could see, the walls of the castle still stood, but it is impossible to tell how bad the situation was from afar. We camped on the overlook, knowing there would be nothing we could do tonight and that the castle was still a half day's walk away.

In the morning Kinterson marshaled his troops, and we began toward the castle along the road. The air here was thick with smoke from all the fires around. Kinterson's men marched in combat formation. Xaddjyk and Kara walked in front of the formation with Kinterson, Halkiir, and me in front of them. Kinterson was talking strategy with Halkiir when we approached where the knights were massing for an assault presumably. The knight in charge came to greet us, although he looked like he had already seen a great deal of action.

"Greetings, Sentinels. I received word that you would be arriving. I was hoping our reinforcements would be here by now, but we have no word on them," the Knight Captain said.

Kinterson looked around at what few knights were present. "How many knights do you have, Captain?"

"Thirty good men. We had over a hundred, but Knight Commander Thyx attempted a frontal assault. This is what's left," the Captain said. His men looked like they had been through a real nasty battle, with a large number of wounded. If he had thirty good men, he had at least thirty wounded men.

"We have to press on to Kan'Varil or the castle will fall. We need your men," Kinterson said. The Knight Captain simply nodded and left to rally his men for the assault. Kinterson gathered us around while we waited for the knights to gather.

"Okay, I don't mean to sound like an ass, but how do we get into the castle? I doubt that we can just ask the marauders to let us in," said one of the soldiers under Kinterson's command. Everyone looked around, obviously trying to figure out a plan.

"Uh, well, I know I'm new here, but when I was trying to get into a place like this, I always looked for a back door. The castle at

Kal'Hinrathos had a secret escape tunnel that allowed careful access inside the walls. Wouldn't this place have one too?" I asked. Everyone looked at me confused and then looked over to Kinterson, who was also confused.

"This, Kinterson, is why I brought her along," Halkiir said, smiling with pride.

"That's good, thief, that's really good, but where would this tunnel even be at? I won't send my people to search all around the castle. There is like sixty miles in every direction."

"Well, if it were me I'd look somewhere around rocky environments or near a lake. I'd put it where you can easily get lost if you were escaping as well as where you won't discover it by accident. Also I wouldn't expect it to be more than four to ten miles away."

"Hey, isn't there a lake with a granite intrusion and high cliff wall just about seven miles northeast of the castle?" one of the other soldiers asked.

"Yeah, Lake Vaeniuu," one of the soldiers said.

"Is there a dock nearby and maybe a river that leads away from the lake?" I said.

"Yeah, there is the River Etimus, leads north and connects to the Lake Syia and Aaomysiir," the soldier replied.

"That's it—that's where I'd put it," I said. The Knight Captain returned just in time for us to formulate a real plan. He had about twenty ragged knights who looked like they have seen some real nasty action.

"These are all the knights that I could assemble. They may look rough, but they are good men, all of them," the Knight Captain said.

"Then let's move," Kinterson said.

We knew that we could not march along the road or risk being seen by the marauders. We had too few knights to risk injury while fighting the marauder patrols. Instead it was decided that we would march in the ravine along the river down to the lake. The ravine was obviously not intended for travel on this scale, and so it took a bit more effort to do so. However, along the ravine we were surrounded by the rock of the upper river bed, which was dry now but would fill during the rainy seasons. Also there was a dense wall of trees between us and the road. Even though the trees were only a few hundred feet thick between us, the forestation was so dense that it was impossible to see more than a couple feet in any direction. We opted to silently march along the river despite the difficulty. The river flowed calmly south from Lake Vaeniuu as a beautiful, crystal-clear stream. Most of the water I had seen before was filled with sand. Never before have I seen water so clear you could see everything through it like perfect glass. Seven miles was a long hike even on a road, but here it would easily take us all day. This was less a problem, as we didn't want to enter the tunnel until after dark anyway. However, the exhaustion of the men was a big concern.

Somewhere about halfway to the lake, the riverbed narrowed, and it was either cliff wall or in the river. It was not practical to follow the cliffs as it rose several feet above the river not far ahead and gave us a greater chance of being seen, so in the river we went. Luckily, the river wasn't very deep, and the soldiers' high boots easily kept their feet dry. Unfortunately I'm too short, and my high boots ended just under the water level, so my boots became little water buckets. The water was so cold I couldn't believe it. Never in my life has anything been this cold. Living in a desert city all my life, the coldest thing I've seen was cold food. In Kal'Hinrathos, even the nights are hot enough to boil an egg. Xaddjyk was standing beside the river and pulled me aside when I reached him. He pulled me out of the river and handed me a new pair of boots that looked longer than mine. I pulled my boots off and poured the water out and removed my soaked stockings and put on the ones that Xaddjyk provided with the boots. Putting the boots on was a bit of a challenge, as they were just higher than my knees and had leather straps on them that went all the way up. As I got the boot on, he tightened the leather straps on the first as I did the second, following what he did. After they were tightened and I stood up, the boots fit so perfectly and were so easy to move in that they had to be made for me. They allowed full movement, but it seemed that they had some armor value as well. There were several places where knives could be attached and appeared to be very functional and pretty comfortable too. After I got my new boots we continued in the river, and this time I kept the water out of my boots, and walking was way easier.

We arrived at the lake not but half an hour before the sun disappeared below the horizon. We began toward the dock but found that there were a dozen or more marauders camped right in our way. Our group was way too heavily armored to swim across to the dock, and the single path leading to it was packed with goons.

"All right, let's take them fast and quiet, men," Kinterson started, but he was interrupted by Xaddjyk, who put his hand up as if motioning for patience. Kinterson said nothing but looked back out to the marauders who received a very unwelcomed surprise. Arrows hailed out of the forest, striking the marauders one by one, always hitting kill shots, and in but a few second they all lay dead on the ground. At this point Xaddjyk stood up and led the way into the clearing himself. We all followed, though some were more cautious than others. One man came out of the forest armed with a bow. One man had killed all these men single-handedly, and Xaddjyk was expecting him. The man was obviously a ranger and wore leather armor with a mask and long cloak. He was armed with his bow and quiver and also with a crossbow on his back, a long sword, and an assortment of other blades and filled pouches on his belt. He stumbled out of the woods, surprised to see Xaddjyk even though Xaddjyk wasn't surprised to see him, not that he'd show it either way.

"Xaddjyk, you crazy bastard," he said as he pulled down his mask. He was a middle-aged man who has a well-trimmed beard of dark black. He was tanned and appears to have seen much action, as evidenced by his scars. The man was smiling and greeted Xaddjyk with a quick one-armed hug and one-armed handshake.

"So, Xaddjyk, it's clear that I received your message, inconvenient as it was, but here I am. So what's going on?"

"Sorry to interrupt another good drunken brawl, but I have a feeling that this is going somewhere we could use some help, so I sent out the word."

"Did you call everyone?"

"I sent word to them all, and they will meet up with us when they can, if they can," Xaddjyk finished, heading back into the camp with the ranger following.

"Everyone, huh? Well, it would be nice to get the old gang together, but I don't like a situation that has you so tangled that you need to bring all the crazies out," he said, laughing slightly. Xaddjyk and the ranger split up in the camp as the ranger went to retrieve his arrows. His arrows were made of some kind of black metal that resembled Xaddjyk's gear. They had the strange etchings carved into the shafts but were not maddening in its design. As he pulled his arrows out of the bodies, it made a disturbing squishing sound as stuff—disgusting in general—oozed out in the arrow's absence. He managed to retrieve every arrow without any of them breaking, including one that went through a man's head and into a tree. Whatever material they were made of, it was not wood.

"Nice shot," Kinterson said as he pulled an arrow from a man's eye, making a disgusting squishing sound. As he pulled the arrow out, the man's eye and his brains kind of followed. Kinterson chuckled and stood up as the brains dripped out.

The ranger came up behind him, taking his arrow with a smile on his face. "Thank you. I do try, sometimes. Name is Hawk, by the way."

"Erik Kinterson," Kinterson replied, unimpressed. "So why are you here? You are not one of the king's men judging by your lack of formality."

"True, I'm not. I'm here because Xaddjyk figured you could use my bow, so here I be."

"Simple as that?" Kinterson asked almost sarcastically.

"Simple as that". The others had been entering the camp slowly and were rummaging through their supplies, looking for anything useful as well as any food they could get their hands on. Lucky for us there was a good fire already started and some kind of pig roasting on a spit. It actually smelled pretty good, and two soldiers, one a Sentinel, the other a knight, had already taken it upon themselves to ensure that it was finished properly. The rest moved bodies and made themselves comfortable, resting before we headed into Kan'Varil. We knew that Kan'Varil's time was running out, but we also knew that we wouldn't be any help if we were hungry and fatigued. We saw a few marauder patrols off in the distance, but they stayed far enough from us that they could not make us. We all sat by the fire as everyone told stories about their service and ate until night had fallen and the sun had disappeared entirely below the horizon. Everyone got a few hours of sleep before we knew we had to move. As I was trying to get some sleep, someone woke me with a shake, and I turned to see who it was. It was Halkiir, who motioned for me to follow him. We walked outside the camp over to the beach of the lake.

"So we need to find this escape tunnel or else we will have a nice assault squad with nothing to assault," Kinterson said, looking off along the cliff side, hoping to sight it.

"Well, if it were me I would look along the cliff probably in an intrusion or a natural cave, anywhere it can't be seen directly from the lake or the road," I said. We walked along the cliffs searching for the exit but found nothing. There were no intrusions and no caves. We couldn't find any particularly good places to put a large hole in the cliff to accommodate a tunnel exit. We searched for hours—well, until the sun was up, when Kinterson was on the brink of giving up. I was sure that there had to be one, but we couldn't find it. We were heading back when I tripped over a stupid burrow and rolled down the hill. The others were asking if I was okay as loudly as they could without risking detection. I was about to yell back when I found the tunnel entrance, coincidentally. We had been looking along the solid cliff face, hoping it was carved directly into the cliff but didn't look at our feet. The designers of Kan'Varil had instead put the escape tunnel under the cliffs and had a ladder that led to the surface. The exit was hidden by the massive underbrush and sealed over by a metal disc that covered the entire entrance.

"Guys, it's here!" I yelled almost without regard for secrecy. They all ran down to me through the underbrush. The tunnel exit was nearer to the lake and was hidden among the trees and bushes that covered the area. It was a wonder that we found it at all. It wasn't obvious because the old dock had been destroyed years ago, and the new dock was placed farther down, but you could still see the stilts that held the old dock up no more than fifty feet from here. Also the massive vegetation would allow a great number of people to move to the water fairly disguised. However, the seal over the top was unlike anything I have seen and had no apparent way to open it. The crest on the seal was that of the old Kan'Varil barony, suggesting that the passage was several hundred years old. It was very probable that it was built during the original construction of the fortress.

"Luck seems to favor you," Kinterson said as he kneeled over, brushing dirt off the seal. His Gauntlet glowed with an unusual blue glow as he touched the seal.

"Not sure what kind of magic is protecting this thing though," Hawk said, standing behind Kinterson, looking over his shoulder.

"I guess. I never cared much for magic, and I didn't think to bring mages in my complement," Kinterson said, standing up and looking up at the Knight Captain with an inquisitive gesture. The Knight Captain was still standing at the top of the hill with his men. He was ushering his men down toward the group and looked down to see the gesture Kinterson was giving and started down the hill himself.

"Sorry, Kinterson, but when the commander tried to push his way into the fortress the mages were first to go. I don't have any mages left under my command." Halkiir had been studying the seal for some time, silently trying to discern the kind of magic behind it.

"This is extremely old magic, possibly older than Kan'Varil even. I don't understand how the architects of Kan'Varil managed to seal this," Halkiir commented.

"Can you open it, Halkiir?" Kinterson asked.

"Possibly, this magic dates back to the Triaegis Empire and thus difficult to remove. However, I might be able to lift the seal momentarily. As soon as we enter, it will seal again. We may not be able to get out this way if we fail," Halkiir said

"I say we go," I said. All the others agreed one by one though you could see the decision wasn't made lightly. You could see the desperation in everyone's faces, except Hawk, who looked far more like he was enjoying the idea of running though a dark and possibly infested ancient tunnels. Halkiir and Kinterson had a worried expression shared between them as though they were giving this a great deal of thought, ensuring that this was in fact the only way. We had no idea where this tunnel would let out at, and we had no idea what the situation in the castle was. We were operating under the assumption that the defenders still held the keep at least and were actively defending against the marauders. Everyone gave the final go-ahead silently, as they truly understood the gravity of the situation we were about to get into. Halkiir drew a strange glyph on the seal with his Gauntlet, which glowed a bright green on the crest and then faded. I could just barely hear some strange mechanism clicking into place. It sounded like a great many clockwork gears spinning into place though magical propulsion. After a short time the gears stopped, and there was a clank that marked that the seal was unlocked. It took Halkiir and Kinterson's combined strength to lift what turned out to be an almost foot-thick metal cone that angled inward slightly. When they dropped it, it didn't bounce and sounded off a single solid sound. It was attached to the opening with a solid-looking hinge. Within the hole was a single ladder that led deep into the darkness that not even the midday sun could pierce.

One of the knights came forward with a torch, dropping it down into the darkness, which fell for over seven seconds before hitting the stone ground and exploding in a small fireball, sending sparks flying. The torch was only burning with the slightest flame.

"Uh, so who goes first?" asked the knight who had earlier dropped the torch.

"That'll be me, of course," Hawk said, almost excited by the prospect as he started down the ladder at a moderately cautious pace.

"I'll go and make sure he doesn't hurt himself," Kinterson said as he started after him. One by one we all had our turn, allowing enough room between us on the ladder. I was near the end but not last down the ladder. I could see at least half a dozen knights and Sentinels above me. I could hear talking in the tunnel below as it echoed through the stone halls, but there were other echoes as well, things I could barely hear. The ground at the bottom was cold, as there was a cold cloud just above the ground that I could feel through my boots. The others before me had already set up torches along the tunnel, showing a clear stone pathway that led through the mountain that turns too often to be able to tell how far it went. The tunnel's stone architecture was sturdy despite the appearance of great age. The masonry work was beautiful with large tiles of whites, blacks, and various shades of gray. The tile patterns were unlike anything I have ever seen in Kal'Hinrathos. It was hard to tell what it was supposed to look like under several centuries of dust and silt blackening the walls. However, despite the tunnel being so close to the lake, there appeared to be no amount of water leaking in, and everything seemed dry. I can hear the echoing of people talking around the corner out of sight.

"Sir, we found several tunnels leading in multiple directions. I have ordered my men to not stray far from the main tunnel until we know which direction we need to head in," one of the Sentinels said.

"Check the walls for designs or symbols that tell us where we are," Halkiir said as he turned to the wall. Everyone turned to the walls, looking for any clue as to where we need to go from here. Unfortunately the silt on the walls was as hard as stone, and they had taken to knives and daggers in an attempt to chip it off. I could hear the chipping away like tiny pickaxes going at mineral deposits. Halkiir was using his Gauntlet at the wall, but even that seemed fruitless.

"Gods above and spirits among, this is useless. We need diamond-tipped picks to get through this. It's like eight hundred years of silt buildup caked on these walls," Kinterson shouted while holding his dagger and turning away.

"There has to be another way to get this shit off," one of the knights said, also abandoning his attempts.

"This place is pretty well designed both structurally and magically. How did all this silt even get in here, let alone stick so resiliently to the walls?" I asked in genuine inquiry.

"Again with the intuitive little scamp. What are you? An architect of magical constructs now?" Kinterson rebuked in a half-sarcastic and half-arrogant tone.

"She might just have a point," Halkiir started before he was interrupted by a strange echo deeper within the tunnels. The sound was strange and unfamiliar. It was echoing from deep behind the dark curtains of shadow that clouded the tunnel's long corridors. Everyone stood in silent wonder, slaves to the strange sound that went unrecognized by all and yet captivated us all the more so. With each new iteration of the sound, it grew louder and more distinct from its mirror echoes that stood to confuse and muddy its peculiar tone. This echo almost demanded us to come and discover what secrets it may be holding. We started out following the loud tone through the tunnels, hoping it would lead us to where we wished to go. We stumbled on through the darkness, cautious and alert. The soldiers in front walked slowly with shields brandished high and with torches held aloft like spears with their light piercing through the darkness. Those in the back were cautious of our flank and held no torches but stood ready, always looking behind us for trouble. However, it was that which was hiding in the shadows that gave me pause, not any silent threat lingering in the darkness behind us. Perhaps this was the idea; perhaps the threat behind us was more prevalent. Yet my mind would not wonder from the strange echoes in the deep. We in the middle held our torches high, vigilant of our surroundings and ready at a moment's notice to drop our light in favor of arms.

As we pressed on, deeper and deeper, closer to the strange sound, the more it sounded unnatural. Its echoes were less prevalent and the sound more clear, and yet more a mystery than ever. It sounded off with the echoes of metal and piercings of steam and was unlike anything we had ever heard. With each step we treaded in silence, waiting for the echoes to guide us closer and deeper into the unknown. We could only imagine what we would find at the source of it. If we had known, we would not have gone at all, and things would have been very different indeed. Xaddjyk and Kara had not entered with us though. I seek their presence like a cloak of safety but found nothing but darkness and fear. We pressed through the darkness for the longest time, following the loudening and ever more unnatural roaring of something great beyond us. Every corner bore the possibility of being the last, and yet the tunnels stretched on and on like an unending labyrinth that had snared us. After walking so long, after so many tunnels that all looked the same, after so much nothingness, it wasn't the strange machination that I feared—it was being trapped forever in the dark and the cold of these tunnels. They seemed to go on until the ends of the world. After seeing nothing for so long, we let our guards down, and that was when when we found what it was we were looking for.

We wandered into a massive circular chamber devoid of light, same as the rest of this forsaken place. We could hear the sound, powerful and before us yet unseen. The room air was uncomfortably hot, as if it was a boiler that we had stumbled into. The echoes were all around us now, loud and deafening like the roar of a waterfall. It was the sound of a great piston hammering with the power of steam smashing into the solid metal and them releasing a wave of steam that hissed through the air. I could hear the turning of gears and cogs that fit together, clinking as they locked. The men spread out into a line formation with their resolve now renewed and shields again held high. They were tired but did not allow it to show even a little. Discipline demanded they stand and ready their arms. As the first of us dropped his torch in favor of a sword, a dim candlelight lit within the darkness. It was dim at first but grew and grew until it was a bright red ring of heated steel. Other parts of the machine began to glow bright as the hammering of the piston and the winding of the gears sped faster and it awoke. Sparks flew from within it, lighting a brazier that burned into magma before our eyes. The wave of heat was so extreme I wanted to faint dead away right there. The light was intense to our eyes, which had grown accustomed to the dark, but the figure was clear before us. Twenty feet tall it stood, a great creature of steel with eyes as red as the desert sun. Strange glyphs etched into his armored shell glowed with red heat as he emerged from the lake of lava unscathed. His every step was an earthquake that shook our line and faltered our will, yet we stood. The metal beast locked eyes with Kinterson, and they stared each other down for but mere seconds before the great beast let out a tremendous roar that sent molten steam so hot it glowed, flying forth at our shield wall. Three men were boiled alive before my eyes, but we deflected it, and the rest survived. We didn't know what to do, and so we foolishly charged in.

I don't know who charged first, but steel blades clashed against the impervious hide of the beast, ringing throughout the room. I saw various spells explode upon his shell uselessly as he sent men flying with every swing. This Clockwork Golem seemed an invincible and indestructible guardian left behind from an age forgotten by the annals of history, so we fled. We broke ranks and ran into whatever tunnel was closest to us, separating into small groups. I didn't know how many had perished but it seemed like many. I saw some of the men who had been sent flying get up or crawl away, but there was no way to be sure how many. Another knight and myself made for the tunnel we entered from and stopped to help a fallen Sentinel who seemed mostly okay, but we couldn't look back to see who else made it. The roars of the Clockwork Golem were so loud I could hear nothing else as we escaped into tunnels it could not follow. For now we were safe, but divided and lost. The gate to Kan'Varil lay just beyond him, I know it. I saw it at the end of the room, but we could not reach it. We could not get into the fortress to help, nor could we make it back through the labyrinth safely. We were trapped between the beast of fire and steel that was this indestructible clockwork golem and the beast of stone and darkness that was the unending labyrinth before us. Hope had faded into the very darkness that now embraced us at every turn. The roars of the golem still echoed throughout the darkness, reminding us that we were going to die down here . . .

CHAPTER 4

TOOLS OF TRADE "HAMMER"

Sometime before we had entered the tunnels, Xaddjyk and Kara had departed even though Hawk came with us. I didn't discover where they had gone until Kara told me what they had gone through when they turned up some time later. As it went, they departed that night while we camped on the surface before coming down into that tomb. They headed east back the way I came, toward the port city of Kal'Hinrathos and the shining seas and dry deserts. I wish I had gone with them, for whatever cesspool Kal'Hinrathos can be, it is still home and a beautiful city in the right parts. I miss the desert heat and the sea air. I don't know how they traveled so fast, but they made it to Kal'Hinrathos by midday when we were just finding the tunnel seal. They came into sight of the great walls of the desert fortress as the gold glistened with the light of the sun and the desert heat distorted the walls in a haze. They came to the city of Kal'Hinrathos not for anything this city itself held, but to take a ship to Januus'Anub the kingdom of sand and gold. There were ships leaving to the deserts every day, as it was the most important trade route in the kingdom for both kingdoms. It brought wealth to Aaomysiir and the kings of Adiin'Ayr. The ship they went on took them to the great city of the sands and home of the gold palace, Kalamothae, the jewel of the east. The ship they were taking belonged to a friend of theirs, which I am inclined to believe is a pirate and corsair and generally bad guy altogether. How they ever met is beyond me. The ship was a triple-mast assault frigate that was, so I hear, more advanced than those used by either navy. Due to many upgrades, probably provided by Xaddjyk, this ship was faster and more maneuverable than its counterparts. This ship adequately named *The Adakar*, which is really obscure and ancient Anubian for a "deathly visage."

The ship waited for them in the slum docks on the outskirts of the harbor, which is rarely traveled by any self-respecting sailor. This is the part of town so bad that not even I ventured here often. It was mostly comprised of decaying slums where the unwanted ended up. It was just inside the outermost walls, and should an invasion occur, these slums would burn in the first attack for sure. Nobody really cares about these outlying districts, and so they are left to rotting decay and crime. The space between the two outer walls is supposed to be a buffer to prevent any fire from siege weapons from entering and damaging the city proper. However, some unwanted persons decided to make this free space their home. The Marquis doesn't care so long as they don't compromise the walls and allows them to exist inside the buffer. Here, there is a cramped city that was built up instead of out. The streets are narrow and crowded, making moving around the "dust town" impossible. The entire area was constantly hit by sandstorms that swept over the outer wall and hit the inner, making it always dusty, hence the name dust town. This was another reason for the two-wall design here. It was strange just how many people were crammed into this narrow makeshift city, trying to live behind walls of stone. I guess it is the perfect place to get lost in the crowd of thousands where guards don't even bother patrolling. The protection of dust town is handled by local crime lords looking for a semblance of order to work in. It was here that Xaddjyk and Kara came to meet their pirate captain hidden within the many unknown faces. In dust town the higher you live, the more powerful you are, which is strange since they are actually in more danger from siege fire and sandstorms, but that is how it is there. The bar they went to was pretty high up and not so crowded. It was made for pirate captains almost exclusively, and so a tense place it must have been indeed. When Xaddjyk entered, he made the same impression he always does—shock and fear. Everyone looked but they dared not say a word.

They went to the farthest and coincidently darkest corner in the shaggy patchwork structure. The outside of this building looked like it was pieced together with scrap wood and metal sheeting that probably drifted from the harbor, and the inside looked pretty much the same. Nothing inside looked as though it fit perfect, and the doors, which were a little better than planked wood panels nailed together, hung from their hinges. There was a strangely sturdy-looking door in the dark corner that looked blatantly out of place among this scrappy dwelling. Kara shunted ahead between Xaddjyk and a barrel table near the back, getting to the door. She rapped on the door, which sounded like it was made of five-inch-thick, strong, solid wood. This door was easily sturdier than any piece in this dive, and yet no one cared to notice, as if it was just a part of the scenery. The door was slightly ajar, revealing only darkness within, but you could hear inaudible sounds within. It took but a second before the slot again closed, and the echoing sounds of great locks could be heard. The locks sounded both heavy and complicated and echoed through the door. After several minutes, the door finally swung open again, revealing only darkness within. Xaddjyk and Kara disappeared inside, and the door slammed shut and the locks were reset. No one looked or even noticed that the door had ever opened. Once inside the door, they walked along a dark hallway, led by a strange magical globe that was levitating in Kara's hand. The hall was long and unlike the rest of dust town looked more like the architecture of the city walls. The bar was directly against the inner wall, so it seemed possible. They walked for several minutes until they reached a similar door at the end of the stone hallway. The locks on this door were the same on this side as they were on the other door and took several minutes to unlock by the cloaked man who had unlocked the first door. Everyone remained silent as they walked through the hall and as they waited for the door to be unlocked.

As soon as the door opened, the sounds of cheerful revelry echoing through wide halls of marble and precious metals heralded a cheerful gathering. When they entered, the lights of the desert sun shined through the marble columns, drawing long dancing shadows that mirrored their dancing counterparts. All the dancers and those in attendance were well dressed in fine silks of vibrant colors and delicate accessories. There were cheerful laughs from jokes told and ears closely heeding every word of stories told. This part of the story I didn't understand when they told it to me. I couldn't understand how two doors and a short hall could lead someone from dust town to the central palace of the Marquis located over five miles away atop of a small granite mountain. Of course Kara only said that the door, the hall, and the man inside are not what they seemed to be. I figure that was as good a reason as any. The grand ball parties held within the Marquis's palace were legendary for both their splendor and their extravagance, and the royal families of every kingdom were known to attend. Although what a pirate would be doing at such an exclusive fête, I can't imagine. I also don't know how he got in. The Marquis held his parties on the veranda of the Kal'Hinrathos Blue Palace. The veranda is near the center of the palace keep at the top of the central palace. This area is among the most defended locations in the whole kingdom. Suffice it to say, no one enters the palace who isn't invited, unless you use a magical door or something.

The veranda was a beautiful piece of architecture with tall marble columns holding up a ceiling of gold and blue stone, glistening with pure crystals that shined in the light and that pour beautiful rainbows across the floor. The veranda had a massive balcony that looked over the city and the sea as the sun set into the east. The setting sun didn't seem to slow the revelries down any as revelers danced across the floor in the dying light. There were a few tables arrayed along the inner walls and near the great columns although most people were on the floor or out on the balcony. However, one such table near the balcony had a single occupant, a well-dressed man who gladly wore a very large feather hat. Xaddjyk and Kara approached the man who was sipping carefully from an elegant goblet made from a piece of sapphire. There was a bottle on the table that was an ornate bottle of carved crystal, possibly purple amethyst. As they approached closer, they could see the intricate carvings. However, it was the smell that stood out the most, a subtle aroma of night and desert rain. Though the smell was subtle once you smelled it, you'd find that you cannot ignore it as it becomes as strong and evident as a desert rainstorm. I knew of this wine before she explained any further. She was describing one of the Almotha or Moon Light Wines. They are the rarest and most treasured of all beverages in existence. They were brewed millions of years ago, perhaps longer. Not much is known about them except that they were brewed using very powerful magic long since forgotten.

These wines are said to be so powerful that they can induce feelings of bliss and even show you memories for a time in the distant past. However, the most mysterious enchantment is that once the bottle is empty, all one would need to do to fill it up is add a drop of spring water under the light of a full moon. No one understands the magic behind these wines, only that they cannot be broken or manipulated in any way. I have heard tales and legends of these but never heard of one in modern times. It's equally confusing how this pirate obtained it; it was probably stolen. He sipped carefully from his sapphire goblet, keeping with the affluent image he was portraying.

"Ah, my friend, always the paranoid critique. I swear we are all beginning to wonder if you are welded into that armor," the pirate said in the most unusual accent. His accent was not the accent that society placed on pirates and seamen in general. His accent was rich, and it seemed to round off all the sounds into a vocal melody and avoided harsh syllables. He sounded like a man of wealth, and his accent was clearly not from these desert lands. His accent actually sounded somewhat romantic and poetic, even if he was talking about something mundane.

"Captain Dus'Pois, always mingling with the heights of society and everything that looks to lock you away for good," Xaddjyk said while pulling the polished wood chair out to have a seat at the table. By the way, his name was not pronounced in the way you might think it should be. I had to ask how it was supposed to be spelled, but it was pronounced *"Duus-pwah"* or something.

"And dear Kara, my word . . . love, you look as stunning as the day I first set eyes on you," the captain remarked at Kara as she too took a seat at the table. "I must of course ask you to dance, if I knew you were the dancing kind, yes? Ha ha."

"I don't think I'm adequately dressed for such a gala as this, I'm afraid," she replied.

"Ah, nonsense, always a beauty you are, the dangerous and mysterious kind, which is the very best kind. Don't you agree, my friend? Ha," the captain said, leaning back in his chair and setting his goblet on the table in front of him. "Ah, how rude of me. Would you care for some? A very good year, this."

"Yes, a very good year. Of course you have no idea what year that might be," Kara said, turning the bottle as if looking for a label.

"No, I suppose not, but aren't they all good years? I have never heard of a compliant from anyone who tasted from this wine or its brothers. Trust me. As you know we are wine people, everyone. We know our wine. Of course the same may be said of you, my dear. We may not know its year of conception, but you probably do know," he continued, following with a short chuckle. Kara picked up the bottle and examined it closely

After a short while, she put the bottle down carefully and said, "One of the Tasalvhains, I believe he only made three. This was his second."

"Good year?"

"Yes, very."

"Ha ha, I knew it. Like I said I have a nose for wine. Anyway, I'm sure that you two did not come to this sand pit for wines alone. What can I do for you?" Captain Dus'Pois asked, leaning forward again and corking the bottle with a shard of crystal that obviously went with it.

"Your ship, Captain. I hear it's the fastest in these waters," Xaddjyk said.

"As I figured, old friend. So where might I be taking you today, and for what bit a treasure do you seek, hmm?" the captain asked, ending with his usual chuckle.

"Kalamothae."

"Ah, the Jewel of the East—just another pit of sand to me, and I can't stand the heat either, but the gold and the actual jewels are too good to pass up, and so here I be and there I go. Though I do long for the days when we traveled the nine seas together, seeking great adventures and a little bit of wealth too. Ha ha . . ."

"Yes, you two did have a tendency to attract trouble," Kara added.

"Ha ha, indeed, but if my memory has not faded from wine, you were there for a lot of the trouble too, no?"

"Have no fear. I suspect that interesting places are just over the horizon," Xaddjyk said.

"Ha, good to hear, my friend. Then let us head for that horizon, no? But first Kalamothae seems to be calling us. Best not to keep a lady waiting, no?" Everyone stood, which went mostly unnoticed because by this time everyone was clearing out anyway, as the sun had almost sunk completely into the great sea in the east. The captain's garb was far more intricate than it appeared while he was sitting, and his hat was unnecessarily big with an unnecessarily big feather in it. He wore almost all white but with a pair of clean, black sailor's boots and several black belts that looked like they ordinarily held pistols. Interesting fact: though pistols and other firearms had been invented by a chemist years ago, many people have rejected the technology due to its faulty record and because they aren't as powerful as magic. Only pirates and other outlaws have embraced the idea because their shot has proven ineffective against modern armor, but sailors rarely wear any. It's a bit awkward since the black powder that allows firearms to function won't work if it's wet.

As everyone was leaving the party, Captain Dus'Pois led the way out of the veranda down an intricate set of stairs leading down from the top of the veranda into the palace proper near the great hall. The ceiling in the palace proper was massive with tall columns. The palace interior was made of red marble embroidered with gold and precious gems. The ceiling was painted blue like the night sky. The great hall was full of people both coming and going. The hall was flanked by heavily armed guards in intricate armor of silver and gold. The voices of all the people in the great hall echoed off the walls, making it hard to hear anything. The captain walked about with ease, and it was clear that most of the nobles here knew him. A man in extremely intricate and ornate clothing of gold and silk, wearing a thin gold crown with large emeralds on it, was standing in the center of the hall, greeting the nobles as they left.

"Ah, Captain Dus'Pois . . . leaving already? Figured you'd stay longer. You usually do," said the man who was flanked by three armed guards.

"Ah, Lord Marquis, I did not see you out on the veranda. I wasn't sure you were even here," Captain Dus'Pois said. The Marquis turned his head to look at some well-dressed noble who was waving the Marquis toward the throne. I'm guessing that the man waving was the seneschal, Lord Baron Amvalkii.

"No, my friend, I've been here, just ridiculously busy. You can't believe how much unrest there is in this this area. We have marauder armies threatening the city, and patrols have been attacked by bandits within the divisionary limits with increasing numbers. I've already ordered double patrols and all naval forces on full alert to prevent enemy ships from getting within the Kal'Hinrathos naval limits as well as protecting the shipping lanes. All my requests for additional forces from Aaomysiir have been ignored," the Marquis explained.

"I didn't realize things had gotten so bad. It has been about a week since we dropped anchor."

"The problems started rather suddenly about a week ago. I'm not sure where this is going, but I don't like it. I have trust in this city to stand against siege, but I'd rather keep the battle away from the walls. I have a feeling that these issues are a symptom of something greater stirring."

"Wow, that sounds like a terribly cliché story, or, uh, is that just me?" Kara added in jest. Everyone looked at her with gazes of both confusion and agreement.

"Wait, I know you, don't I? You look familiar," the Marquis said to Kara.

"Uh, it's possible. We do a lot of traveling, and we have been here before, I think." In the meantime, Xaddjyk, who had apparently disappeared some time ago, just approached from somewhere within the crowd. As he approached, he was fairly hard to miss, as he was taller than the others in the crowd. Also everyone seemed to get out of the way as he waded through.

"Xaddjyk, we were just conversing about the situation in the march . . ."

"Xaddjyk, well, I wasn't informed that you were in Kal'Hinrathos. If I knew I would have welcomed you Prelate. Figures you wouldn't inform us of your presence. That and I'm not even going to ask how you made it into the palace keep without anyone noticing," the Marquis said in a rather annoyed tone. "And you, now I know where I know you, Paladin."

"Oh, Paladin, that's good, better than some of my other reputations," Kara said.

"Hang around this guy long enough, and I'm sure you will collect several disreputable stories."

"You have no idea."

"Well, I have *important* stuff that needs doing. Feel free to drop by whenever you want. Oh, and, Xaddjyk, drop by whenever. You do anyways."

"Marquis, Captain, the situation is escalating, and we need to get to Kalamothae. This situation grows more dire with time," Xaddjyk said.

"Of course. I already sent word to my men. My ship should be ready already. We can leave whenever you want."

"Good, Kara. Head to the ship with Captain Dus'Pois. I have to obtain a necessary component."

"Yes, sir. I will gather everything we brought with us and get them loaded on the ship. I will also make sure the ship is ready to leave, just in case we have to leave in a hurry." Xaddjyk looked over to Kara with a strange look, stopping dead as he was walking away.

"What? The last time you 'acquired' something we needed, you basically stole it," Kara said quietly, almost whispering and shrugging. Captain Dus'Pois laughed in the background behind Kara, shaking his head. Xaddjyk looked at both of them shrugging in a "what" kind of way. Xaddjyk disappeared deeper into the palace as Kara and Captain Dus'Pois left out the keep's main gate, heading toward the harbor. The path out of the keep is a strange degradation of society. With each step from the keep, everyone gets poorer and poorer. The city is built in mass districts that separate different societal classes within Kal'Hinrathos. The system seems wrong, but the city was expanded several times and each time a wall was built to protect it. The final product is a segregated city with multiple walls leading into the center of the city where the palace is.

The innermost, and obviously most secure, portions of the city are where the heights of society live. The outer layers of the city are where the poor primarily live near the outer wall, and of course the dust in between the walls. In order to get to the harbor from the keep, you must pass from the Palace District, the Keep District, the Diamond District, the Gold District, the Castle District, the Tower District, the Bastion District, and finally the Harbor District. During the construction of the city, the palace and wealthier parts of the city were to keep the palace district away from the bay for fear of naval assault. The main Keep District is also far enough inside the city as to be protected from land assault from any side.

The first district was the Palace District and is located almost exactly in the center of Kal'Hinrathos guarded by over a dozen walls. The Palace District is a combination of extremely decorative buildings made of rich marble and embroidered with gold and jewels. The center of the plaza just inside the main gate was a massive crystal fountain that you had to pass every time you entered the district. There were also various other fountains scattered around the Palace Plaza. The buildings were connected by large covered walkways and intricate gardens. The gates and doors in the district were reinforced and yet ornately carved of dark metal. The walls surrounding the Palace District are taller than any of the other wall sections standing high above the city.

Once outside the district, the design of everything changes drastically. The Keep District is far different than any of the other districts, as it's purely a military district. The district is small, smaller than any of the other districts and simply encircles the Palace District and contains the Kal'Hinrathos Castle and the primary military barrack and armory. The city's entire main military infrastructure was focused within the military Keep District. The walls here were the thickest and strongest in the city, designed to defend the keep and the palace. The Lord's Road, which leads to the keep into the palace for the city proper, was highly decorative, attempting to hide the fact that it leads right through to the military keep. The Lord's Road was surrounded on both sides by high walls and two gates that lead into the keep from the road.

Passing through the city was a nightmare; every district was crowded even as the sun was setting. The districts inside the primary castle walls as well as the Trade District near the land entrance of the city were busy in all hours and were, as a result, extremely well lit. Even hurrying through the city and avoiding the bazaars, and thus crowds, still took over an hour just to get through all the gates into the harbor districts. Now the city may be fairly active at all hours of the day and night, typically; most of the through traffic is done during the day. The harbor, however, is always busy. Hundreds of tons of cargo pass through the harbor at all hours as hundreds of ship come and go. The harbor of Kal'Hinrathos accommodates ships from all across the main land, Nubia, and all across the sea from the Aegis Empire. Passing through the harbor was dangerous with all the moving cargo to and from ships in the docks. The harbor where people dock their ships for long-term mooring is farther near the mouth of the bay away from the cargo exchange of main harbor. I know the Harbor District well, having lived near there most of my life. The massive and confusing blur of people and cargo made it easy to remain hidden and anonymous. To be honest, they should have taken me. I would have rather spent my week in the deserts of Kal'Hinrathos and Kalamothae instead of in dark, cold tunnels in the bowels of the earth.

Navigating the harbor is complex, as stacks and pallets of cargo are scattered about. If it took them an hour to get to the harbor, it took them at least another hour to get around the harbor to where *The Adakar* was moored. Now I understand that getting a ship ready to sail actually takes some time, but Dus'Pois's crew seemed to know he was coming and already had the ship ready to leave. The ship was perfectly lit, and you could see the deckhands scrabbling across the deck and up the rigging. A tall, dark man was waiting at the bottom of the gangplank. He wore fancy clothing like the captain and was obviously pretty high ranking.

"Ah, Captain, we have been waiting for you," the man said as the captain approached the gangplank.

"Good to hear, Ambrax. We need to cast a line immediately. And where is Emily?" the captain said while walking up the gangplank, looking around.

"Captain, she said that she was dealing with the other part of your plan. To be truthful, I have no idea where she went. Of course she never tells me anything either way," Ambrax said, following Captain Dus'Pois and Kara up.

"Kara, feel free to stand wherever. My men will take care of everything. They are quite good at this actually," Captain Dus'Pois said as he headed for the wheel. "Ambrax, set course for the Collegium at the Island of Kaaliuum." Ambrax headed down the stairs to the main deck, shouting orders to the deckhands and boatswains. Within moments, the gangplank was withdrawn and the ship was unmoored and pushed off from the dock; and the ship began to drift into the bay before the captain ordered a half sail and the ship picked up speed very quickly, leaving the harbor behind, passing ships both coming in and leaving. They headed out of the bay toward an island fairly distant from the mainland. Despite being distant, you could see the Collegium high tower looming over the horizon. They sailed through the night, making excellent time getting to the island. As they grew closer to the island, you could see that the forests and the structures of the Collegium became more and more visible. You could see lights from lanterns along the shore and within the buildings as you grew closer and even students and other mages moving about. They were heading toward the fortifications of Kaaliuum, which was a fortified stone tower that had the island's lighthouse and had high walls.

"All right, Ambrax, take the wheel and sail us along the edge of the fortifications near the wall. Get us as close to the walls as you can, and watch out for the sandbar. Don't beach my ship, Ambrax," Captain Dus'Pois said, heading down to the main deck near the edge, facing the fortifications. "Ambrax, sea hook, and then Starfall maneuver!" he yelled as the ship skimmed past the fortified island. The ship was still traveling at half sail, turning to sail right next to the island without even slowing down. Everyone prepared for something. As the ship passed parallel to the wall, the lighthouse erupted into a fireball, sending glass and wood raining down on *The Adakar*. With this Captain Dus'Pois threw a knotted rope into the water as the ship sail by. A few seconds later the line was tugged, and the deckhands reeled the rope in with a female pirate with an extremely big smile. She wore more traditional pirate garb with thigh-high leather boots, tight pants, and a long leather sailor coat with the sleeves rolled up to the shoulders with gold and silver bracelets on her arms. She wore thin, leather, fingerless gloves with six assorted rings on her thumbs, left index and ring fingers, and right index and middle fingers. She wore a very nice black leather tricorne with three golden rings pierced on the left edge and two large, colorful feathers. Her black hair was braided with an assortment of beads, rings, and cords. The deckhands reeled her onboard, dripping with water with a large, empty bag strung across her shoulder.

"Ah, Emily, I was wondering where you went. Have fun, no?" Captain Dus'Pois asked, looking over at his first mate, smiling. She smiled, shrugging the water off her coat, and threw the empty bag at the arms master, who had come on deck from the armory below.

"Well, that was fun. One can never blow shit up enough," Emily said, brushing sand off her boots. As she was cleaning off her boots, she pulled several sticks of dynamite from ring hooks on the back of her boots. "Oops, where were these when I was setting up my show?" she said. Captain Dus'Pois shook his head and adjusted his hat.

"Ambrax, take the ship over to the Collegium Magus Tower, same as before." Emily headed toward the stern up to the wheelhouse where Ambrax was steering the ship along the coast of the island still at half sail. They sailed toward the rear of the island where the great tower loomed over the island. *The Adakar* got close to the tower with battle mage guards yelling at the ship and chasing it down along the island wall. They got as close as they could with the sandbars, and everyone was looking up, waiting for something. At the top of the tower, Xaddjyk decided it would be quicker to simply jump off. He fell through the air, landing seamlessly on the deck with a large, ornate staff. As soon as he landed on deck, the captain ordered full sail and for the ship to head out to deeper seas to which the crew quickly and efficiently complied, getting the ship out away from the island toward Kalamothae.

"So tell me, Xaddjyk, what did you 'borrow' this time? Something that is going to cause problems, no doubt, no?" Captain Dus'Pois asked, smiling and crossing his arms. Xaddjyk lifted the ornate staff and tossed it to Captain Dus'Pois, who didn't know what to make of it.

"It's a staff, perhaps valuable. What of it?" Emily asked, examining it. Kara came down from the wheelhouse to greet Xaddjyk.

"Oh, Kara, you should really consider wearing something less, well, cumbersome, you know," Emily said to Kara as she walked by. As Kara passed, it was extremely obvious that Kara was noticeably taller, or it was her heeled boots, not sure which.

"Isn't that Arch Mage Tyykon's staff? Uh, this isn't good, Xaddjyk. I mean, you've appropriated some pretty outlandish stuff over the years, but this is really, really bad," Kara said, taking the staff from Emily.

"Um, an explanation would probably be appreciated, no?" Captain Dus'Pois interrupted with a look of confusion.

"Well, Arch Mage Tyykon was the Arch Mage of the old Tower of Ilchaan. After the tower was destroyed, he built the Collegium here at Kal'Hinrathos back when it was just a fortress. Tyykon Ilchaan's staff was said to have originally been forged for a Triaegis emperor and held untold powers. Tyykon himself used the staff to bring the island the Collegium is built on from the bottom of the sea. The Arch Mages of the Collegium have had the staff locked in a magical vault for hundreds of years protected by some of the most powerful magical wards in the world," Kara explained.

"Pretty much," Xaddjyk said, taking the staff from Kara. It's also the key to where we are going." After the colorful explanation, everyone manned their posts and the ship maintained its speed and headed racing for the horizon. The ship was swift, making unbelievable time, ripping through the waves to the southeast.

As the sun began to rise to the stern of *The Adakar*, the sun glared off the gloss of the decks on the fifth day of their journey and illuminated the great city of Kalamothae in the distance. The golden towers of Kalamothae glared in the light of the sun, making the horizon shine and glitter, giving away the city far before it was openly visible. By the light of midmorning they were in sight of the great city of sand and gold, Kalamothae. From what I've heard, Kalamothae is pretty similar to Kal'Hinrathos but is far more ornate and elaborate. As they approached the city there were no less than fifteen Janubian heavy frigates on patrol around the bay as well as a dreadnought anchored in the bay near the harbor with its broadside cannons welcoming everyone to the city. Apparently, the Kalamothian leader Prince Aalmakiin was also taking precautions with the rising troubles cropping up everywhere. Prince Aalmakiin was taking the visual "bring it on" method of maintaining peace on the seas. *The Adakar* came into the harbor and moored in the bay's harbor away from the central trade channel and docked near the private part of the city. The docking authority was already waiting as *The Adakar* dragged into the harbor. The dock authority consisted of four ornately dressed men. The first was obviously a city official, and the second was some kind of assistant carrying a large book, probably the official's logbook. The two other men were heavily armored janissaries obviously there to deal with incongruities. The ship pulled into the dock perfectly, and the gangplank was lowered, and the officials waited quietly on the boardwalk. Captain Dus'Pois was first down the gangplank, followed by his first mate, Emily; and after her, Xaddjyk and Kara and the rest took care of the ship.

"Welcome to Kalamothae, Captain. I need to see your registration and you manifest," the official said with an authoritative voice. Captain Dus'Pois already had a folded leather-bound parchment registration with wax seal containing a special character. I knew a man who did these seals, and each seal is unique per year and are used to confirm the date it was registered. I'm guessing by the look on the official's face that what was on the registration was not what he was expecting. The seal dated last year, but *The Adakar* was registered as an Aegis Imperial Privateer and bore the Imperial Seal of the Aegis Empire. Once he saw the registration, the official closed his logbook, handed the registration back, and walked away without another word.

"Ha, that never gets old no matter how often I use it, though I am going to need to renew my registration soon, if you don't mind, my friend," Captain Dus'Pois said, rolling his registration up and tossing it up to Ambrax, who disappeared into the deck. Xaddjyk passed the captain along the boardwalk, smiling with the staff he "borrowed" over his shoulder. Kara scooted past the captain and Emily to join Xaddjyk further down. Shortly after, Captain Dus'Pois and Emily followed, giving a last glance to the deckhands.

"Xaddjyk, where are you going? I doubt entirely that what you are looking for is here." Captain Dus'Pois asked, catching up. "Well, at least, tell me how long we will be waylaid here. I need to know how many drinks I have to order—and charge you for . . . ha ha."

"Awhile, I'm afraid. We need to head deep into the desert for what we need," he replied, looking back but not slowing down. "I have already set everything up. We just need to meet up with our caravan and head out of the city."

"Where are we heading exactly?" Kara asked.

"Day's End," Xaddjyk said.

"Wait, you're looking for Bastion's Black Forge? Ugh, I hate the desert," Kara remarked, rubbing her head.

"Well, I'm confused. Sometimes I think you too have been around just a little too long to have heard of all this weird stuff no one else has," Captain Dus'Pois said, shrugging behind them.

"Bastion was a genius and master architect during the golden age of the Triaegis Empire. He was behind most of the technological and magical breakthroughs that kept the empire in power for a millennia. Most of his designs were forged in a secret fortress deep in the desert called Storm Rock. At its center was Bastion's Black Forge, which was a massive magical forge that was built on a font of magic. Of course, ironically, Storm Rock was consumed by a massive sandstorm that buried everything around the time of the fall of the empire. Now everyone just calls the area Day's End. The Black Forge has been lost and buried ever since, and the area of Day's End is mostly just a caravanner's story

"Sounds profitable. Of course you would never empower others for mere money—a shame, really, but understandable I suppose," Captain Dus'Pois said. "Well, have fun in the desert. I'll go find some fine wine. Oh, and do we need to prep for a quick escape?"

"Shouldn't be necessary this time."

"Can't steal from the dead, am I right? I get it fair enough. See you soon, unless you die. Ha ha. Wouldn't that be funny? Ha ha," Captain Dus'Pois said, waving and walking away into the richer part of Kalamothae. Xaddjyk and Kara headed into the Trade District, having to wade through the thick crowd of people. The largest bazaar in the city was not far from here, and the crowds were ridiculous. I guess for his purpose the crowds suited him, even if they both stood out. They headed through the bazaar and through the crowded and narrow streets of the city, heading toward the outer gates, where, presumably, the man they were to meet was still waiting with his caravan. The crowds made moving around difficult, much like Kal'Hinrathos, but with even narrower streets. They arrived pretty early in the morning, but it took most of it to get through the crowds and make it to the gates. Here there were two short desert wagons and a group of men waiting. They had camels to pull their wagons and were well stocked for a long expedition into the desert. It was clear that they were waiting for more than just Xaddjyk, probably a trade caravan to Tala'Kar on the opposite coast. I haven't heard much about Tala'Kar except that it is a trade city that trades with the Aegis Empire and is more of a citadel than trade port. I also hear that the city is controlled jointly by the Nubian principalities and the Aegis Imperial Military and has a joint military garrison, but I don't know why. I guess it doesn't matter since Xaddjyk and Kara weren't going that far and were following the Moonpaths only so far.

"Ahh, Xaddjyk, you are actually early. I had expected you late, crowds are murder on one's schedule to be sure," the caravan leader said, standing among the other caravan runners. "I must say your timing is rather impeccable. The other trade carts are almost prepped. We can leave in a few minutes, and we got what you asked for. These should fit over your armor. I must admit I cannot see why you would want to wear armor in the desert. You know it can get to over a hundred and thirty degrees out there? Perhaps more?" the caravan leader asked, handing them two large desert cloaks. The cloaks were a sandy tan color and were hard to spot from the sand. They were of fine make despite the dirty look and were cut and stitched professionally.

"I must admit, I'm glad to have you along. Those damn corsairs have been getting worse as of late. They have been raiding every caravan they can get their hands on," the caravan leader said as they headed out of the main gate. The gates are kept open to allow people from the outskirt towns and villages along the rivers to come to trade at the market. The gates were massive steel doors and were flanked by dozens of guards watching over everyone as the came and went. The caravan leader led his people out of the city, where the rest of the trade caravan was waiting. The rest of the caravan consisted of several long wagons and a contingent of six well-armed, if lightly armored, guards.

"How bad has it gotten?" Kara asked.

"Bad. The major principalities are guarding as much area as they can, but out in the dunes there is nothing to stop the corsairs from raiding as they please. The Tala'Kar run is one of the worst. It's a long time in between civilization."

"Doesn't the Advent's Templar Wardens guard the roads to Tala'Kar?" Kara continued.

"They do the best they can, far better than any of the desert princes or their collective armies do. Tala'Kar is crawling with Templars, and they do a good job guarding the roads leading to the city as well as rooting out and destroying corsair holdouts, but they can't guard all the roads all the time. They keep lookouts for caravans and escort them back when they can, but we still need to get to their perimeter first. I heard where in the desert you are leaving us, and it's pretty close to where we can meet up with a group of Templars. We are glad to show you the way and share our supplies in exchange for the extra protection, my friends."

"Well, don't worry, we'll keep an eye out for you. Try and keep the caravan out of trouble," Xaddjyk replied, putting his cloak on to keep the sand from getting in his armor. As they walked along the road, the civilization around them got more and more scarce as city became villages and villages became sparse settlements and then nothing but dunes. The farther they got from Kalamothae, the smaller the patrols got and the fewer there were. They traveled for a long time over a week, deep into the dunes following the Moonpaths traveling at night and camping during the day in heavy tents. I hear the desert is exactly as advertised—130-plus degrees, powerful sandstorms, and dry, scorching air. I love it in Kal'Hinrathos, but the dunes are way too inhospitable for me. Over a week in the desert is fairly hard to imagine, especially having to do it regularly back and forth. Most of the trip went pretty well and happily uneventful, but naturally that couldn't last. About two weeks into the desert they were bogged down by a sandstorm that blew in from the north, pretty much stopping all travel. They already lost a whole night of travel, and by the way it was starting to look like they were going to lose another night if the storm didn't stop soon. It was already after midday, and despite the storm it was still ridiculously hot and unbearable with all the sand in the air. The visibility was about half as long as your arm, and all you can hear was the roaring wind. The guards were about, looking for trouble, but it was pretty much useless. Xaddjyk and Kara were in the main pavilion with the caravan leader enjoying a drink and wasting time mostly.

"I hate these damn storms. My schedule is all blown to hell now. The problem with this place is when you get one storm, there are always more—they never stop at just the one," the caravan leader said, sipping from a large canteen.

"We are getting pretty close to where we need to be. I'm not surprised to see such storm activity near here," Xaddjyk said, standing near the central table, looking at his map, which was similar to the map Kinterson used but was far more advanced. On his map the terrain actually popped out of the cloth, giving it height off the table. More so, he was able to move the focus of the map, making it show a larger or smaller area and even panning to other areas. Like Kinterson's map, it showed various movements of both the caravan and other military units far off. The map was shifting strangely due to the sandstorm, but it was pretty clear. There were also several landmarks that were clearly not there anymore—who knows how long ago those landmarks disappeared. It's clear that he was using several ancient landmarks to pinpoint Storm Rock. There were small fluttering washes of color around the camp that looked almost like troop movements. You couldn't tell because of the sandstorm, but Xaddjyk knew.

"Tok, I suggest getting your men ready. Looks like we might have company," Xaddjyk said, looking up from his map. Kara grabbed her spear, getting up from her seat on the opposite end of the pavilion and walking over to the map table. Tok the caravan leader also got up quickly, partially confused at what he was talking about.

"What are you talking about? You think they will attack during the storm?" Tok said, looking at the map and back to Xaddjyk. Before Xaddjyk was able to get a word out, there was a roar of screaming and commotion outside that sounded like horses rushing in. Tok was the first outside, having rushed out and grabbing his scimitar and buckler shield. Outside the caravan guards were clashing with corsairs on horseback, and two of the guards were already either dead or incapacitated. The rest of the guards were faring poorly, as they were severely outnumbered and were at the disadvantage of not being on horseback. Most of the civilians were taking cover under the long wagons, trying to keep out of the fight as the guards battled the corsairs. The sandstorm made it difficult to keep track of them as they rode in and out of sight. Tok tried to battle the corsairs as best as he could but found himself only on the defensive against them. Xaddjyk and Kara followed him out into the battle but were immediately set upon by several warriors from multiple directions. The first warrior who attacked Kara from behind found himself dead when her spear implanted through his throat, knocking him clear of his horse. He was dead in an instant, but his death didn't deter his comrades any.

Tok was holding his ground against several warriors and knocked one man clear of his horse with his buckler but was unable to finish the job due to a half-dozen others rushing every which way. Kara had a unique advantage over Tok and Xaddjyk with her spear easily dispatching corsair cavalry as they foolishly approached. She was able to either spear them or dismount them with the spear's bladed hook. After about five, they kept away from her, instead attacking Tok and his men. Xaddjyk waded through the storm mostly unopposed. I'm guessing his armor has a symbolic feature useful as an attack deterrent. One fool did try to attack him from behind; he pulled the typical Xaddjyk move. He grabbed the man's scimitar as he passed, pulling him from his horse and then stomping on his head, making a queasy squishing sound. He then "disposed" of the borrowed sword by throwing it into the storm; its impact was sounded by a corsair having been hit. An amazing throw to be sure, but not beyond the ordinary for Xaddjyk. He just walked normally, obviously unafraid. They caused a lot of chaos but only for a few minutes until the storm started dying down, and then they simple disappeared. Tok was still battling two of them and was actually doing a pretty good job. He was clearly a skilled fighter and was doing a fair job holding them at bay, not to mention having been able to dismount them in the first place. Xaddjyk approached from behind the first and grabbed his own knife from his belt and buried it deep into the base of his skull. The second was distracted by his friend's death, which gave Tok the opportunity to overhand slash him.

Though most of the corsairs had already disappeared, there were still horses without riders wandering aimlessly around the outskirts of the caravan camp. There were several bodies littering the ground, and all were those of the corsairs. The yells of pain from the wounded filled the air with the early stench of death from the fallen. Tok's men were seeing to their own, as no surviving corsairs remained. Xaddjyk kneeled over one of the bodies of the corsairs and analyzed both his weapons and armor. Upon removing the thick desert shroud, sets of fine armor of gold and red were revealed. His weapon was a sharp and perfectly crafted golden sword. Whilst rummaging through the dead corsair's stuff the corsair grabbed Xaddjyk's arm, forcing out a sentence in a strange dialect before falling back down dead. Xaddjyk raised his eyebrow before scrapping the corsair's hand off his arm and then poking him, making sure he was actually dead this time.

"What did he say? I've never heard a language like that before. It isn't Nubian nor is it ancient Nubian," Tok stated, standing behind Xaddjyk.

"It's Nyrian. That hasn't been a spoken language since the Triaegis Empire ruled. Guess these desert insects learned it some twenty or so thousand years ago before the empire was collapsed. I guess they must have been speaking and passing the language down from generation to generation," Xaddjyk explained, standing up.

"You seem to know an alarming amount about the ancient empire. I didn't have you pegged as a scholar with all your weapons and frightening demeanor," Tok said with a fairly confused and awed tone.

"Tok, my friend, it's time we parted ways. These people are probably after us, and without us in your group they should leave you alone. It's not far, perhaps three nights to the Templar lines where you should be able to get an escort the rest of the way to Tala'Kar, another week and half journey," Xaddjyk said, having grabbed his stuff from the caravan wagon.

"I am sad to see you go, Kara, Xaddjyk, but I can understand. These men Kataal and Dahlik are the guides I found in the city per your request; they know the desert and should be able to get you to and from wherever you are headed." Two men in desert cloaks that had been traveling with the caravan but that no one ever paid any attention to stepped forward with packs of their own, already ready to go.

"Please, my friends, we have set aside extra supplies of water and rations for you to take. I only hope it is enough," Tok said, walking to the supply wagon. He had large bundles of supplies specially wrapped and left untouched in the wagon. They were wrapped in such a way that they could easily be stored in a pack without letting either sand or water ruin the rations inside. The bundle was fairly large and likely contained dried breads and salted meats, probably pork. The supplies would likely last a couple weeks if rationed properly. There were also two large canteens, one for each of them, as well as a large animal-skin water sack for reserve water and refills. The sack was too large and unwieldy to drink from directly. It just stored the reserve water to refill their canteens. Xaddjyk and Kara both stored the supplies provided inside their travel packs that they wore on their backs along with their other supplies, such as their bedrolls, whatever food and water supplies they already had, navigation equipment, and other supplies one would need to explore the desert.

They waited for nightfall before they left, using what was left of the day to properly prepare for their journey into the deep desert. When night finally fell, the caravan was prepared to continue northeastward toward Tala'Kar while Xaddjyk, Kara, and the two scouts Kataal and Dahlik headed into the north and the east into the deepest reaches of the desert. These dunes were known as the Desolate Sea and for good reason. No one has ever ventured far into the sea and returned. According to Kara, it has pretty much been this way for a really long time even before Bastion. In fact Bastion's Black Forge was constructed there to avoid the prying eyes of others, even among the empire. The Desolate Sea was said to be over two thousand square miles of sand with no source of water or civilization anywhere within. The caravans from Kalamothae to Tala'Kar must pass through a section of the Desolate Sands as they travel through the heart of the Nubia and so Xaddjyk and Kara had a head start to the center of the sands. Of course the location of the fortress was unknown, and it has been empty for ten or twenty thousand years, probably buried too, which makes things more interesting. However, Xaddjyk, with the "borrowed" staff, headed into the northeast and into the heart of the desert.

For three days they walked further and deeper throughout the nights and most of the days, taking a few hours to rest and eat before continuing. They headed always into the northwest until sand was all they could see. Xaddjyk and Kara are not talkative company, and so the walking was probably silent and boring. I don't know if they knew where they were going or were simply walking, hoping to see something over the horizon. Three nights in, they were walking near a small cliff wall of rock, standing against the tides of sand. The cliff dropped only twenty or thirty feet down but was an adequate shield against the wind that whipped out of the west. They walked close to the cliff wall, trying to stay out of the wind and the sand blowing over it. The full moon's light illuminated the dunes almost as brightly as the sun did in the day, allowing a full visibility of the desert. The roaring of the wind was so loud that the sound of horses went almost unheard. However, Kataal caught the sound on the wind and stopped the group, saying nothing, just listening. His message was quickly understood as the others in the group picked up the sounds in the wind too. Xaddjyk climbed the cliff wall in an attempt to see over and spot the horses. He was looking straight into the wind and sand, but even still the dust storm of a great many horses was clearly visible in the distance heading into the northeast.

"What do you see, Xaddjyk?" Kara asked, looking up at him to his left. He said nothing and simply put his hand out, rubbing his index, middle finger, and his thumb three times and opening his hand, waiting for something. Kara clearly got the message as she started rummaging through her pack until she found a spyglass carefully wrapped in dark cloth to hide its otherwise golden design. She dropped it into his hand, and he opened it and peered through it into the distance. With it he could clearly see the horses and the familiar shapes of the corsairs heading in the same direction that they were heading.

Xaddjyk looked down to Kara and the others tossing the spyglass to Kara, saying, "Rats always know the way. Follow the horses."

"You sure they are heading to the same place you are?" Dahlik asked as Xaddjyk jumped down form the cliff wall.

"There are a lot of horses in that group," Xaddjyk simply said. Dahlik shrugged, confused, and was clearly about to say something before Kataal interrupted.

"Horses are not desert animals. They will need a lot of water, and if someone built a fortress out here somewhere, they would also need water. It's a safe bet that whoever they are, they are using the same water source that the fortress once used." Xaddjyk nodded in agreement and started out. They followed the cliff for several more hours until morning was upon them, and they were at the end of the cliff as it met a large rock protruding from the sand a hundred feet or more into the air like the peak of a buried mountain. They climbed up, tracking the horses from higher ground. Their trail was covered by the sand, but the dust cloud they created as they moved was still visible. They had traveled through a canyon to the other end of a large mountain. On horseback they had to travel through the canyon and around the mountain, but on foot Xaddjyk and the others merely had to climb down to the canyon walk across and climb up the adjacent mountain. By the time they reached the other mountain, however, it was already midday and the air was scorching. The climb was difficult, especially in the heat, and was slow; but they made it up despite several near falls along the way. Once they climbed around the mountain, what they saw was unavoidable and captured the eye instantly. A massive fortress stood within a near circular gap between high peaks on all sides. The fortress was built into the mountains and cliffs and filled the area around the central chasm with high walls and towers all made of a red stone unlike anything I have ever seen. The walls of Windrift were made of a faded orange, like the desert sun, but these walls were as red as blood. Kataal and Dahlik stood in absolute awe before the fortress hidden so completely from the world. The mountain peaks were not that tall and were actually too small to be considered mountains, but the fortress followed them deep into a large chasm. The ground of the fortress was far below the desert floor, suggesting that either the fortress was built here on purpose or perhaps the desert has risen in the twenty thousand years since this fortress was used.

Large sand falls flowed into the chasm from several points around the peaks. There were strange pipes and other machines of an unknown design and purpose. They crisscrossed along the mountain and the walls of the fortress and into various holes in the walls. Several massive pipes came from deep inside the chasm into the fortress. The pipes and machinery were made of a golden-red metal and could be seen in almost every corner of the fortress. The climb down to the fortress floor wasn't half as difficult as it was to climb up to the mountain, as there were traveled stone paths all around the inner side of the peaks. The paths were fairly rough, as though they were carved out of the rock for rare travel. They weren't perfectly cut and were clearly not intended for regular travel, but they seemed safe enough if you were cautious. These paths wound around the inner chasm and led down into the keep's outer courtyard. There were pipes and machines along the paths, which were likely the reason the paths were there in the first place. They descended into the fortress and onto the outer walls, at which point it was a simple matter of entering into the central courtyard. The fortress was eerily empty and yet in extremely good condition considering it was thousands of years old. The masonry was extremely advanced but clearly foreign and unfamiliar. There were several entrances into the fortress around the edges into the mountain face. There was one more inside a building in the center of the courtyard that led into the city proper.

The fortress's facilities were located within the mountains around the courtyard, leaving all the area beneath the fortress for Bastion's city. According to Xaddjyk, Bastion's underground city held a population comparable to the greatest surface cities of the modern age with something like a hundred and some thousand people. I can't imagine living underground, but I guess different times. The descent into the city consisted of a series of stairs made from a combination of stone and golden steel. There were lanterns that held some kind of blue crystal within. These crystals, like the rest of the city, appeared to be all but dead. They gave off faint blue light barely enough to see, especially given the hazardous nature of the city. Kataal and Dahlik lit torches in order to provide better illumination than the crystal troches could manage. Kataal was up front with Xaddjyk while Dahlik took up the rear, falling slightly behind. With the torches you could see that the city was built of a more grayish stone than that of the fortress outside, suggesting that the city was actually carved instead of constructed. You could see other machines like giant pumps along the walls as well as gears and pistons that served an unknown purpose. This technology could be seen everywhere as they descended deeper and deeper into the city. As they explored the city, it became clear that the technology was present throughout, and it seemed that the city itself may in fact be one massive machine built by

Bastion for some mysterious reason. However, despite all the advanced culmination of magic and technology, the city seemed to be dead, as none of the devices were functioning. The gears and pumps of the city had long since fallen silent, and it appeared that they had been for a long time.

"What is this? I have never seen anything like this city before." Kataal asked, examining the odd technology built into the walls. He was examining a massive series of clockwork gears that operated a massive piston device that conquered an entire section of wall. The pistons came out of the floor, but it was unclear how far down they went.

"Bastion was a savant in both his magical knowledge and his technological expertise. We can expect that this place is something extraordinary. Even more he kept this place a secret even from his own empire, so it must have been extremely important," Xaddjyk explained as they continued. The corridors were wide and tall, too wide and tall for the torches to properly illuminate, and a lot of the details were lost due to low light. The metals from the various machines were a sort of bronze gold and were fairly muted and didn't reflect light, making the corridors seem bigger and hard to navigate.

"From what I know about ancient imperial locations, most of them are in fairly ruined states. Why aren't these?" Dahlik asked.

"Well, like Xaddjyk said, Bastion kept this place a secret and it is fairly hidden. It's likely that during the collapse of the Triaegis Empire this place was safely hidden away," Kara explained further. As they traveled it was clear that the city was extremely well preserved and looked as though it was built recently despite the two millennia worth of dust and sand over everything. The city was massive, and yet it was clear that Xaddjyk knew where he was going by the markings and signs located on the walls. The signs were written in a language that the guides and even Kara couldn't understand. Their description reminded me of being trapped in the tunnels, and it makes me feel very claustrophobic. They said that the corridors of the city were actually very roomy, and there were large open chambers all practically everywhere around the city. However, the whole city was basically one giant labyrinth, especially if you couldn't read the signs. At one point they entered a grand chamber with an open wall that looked out into the massive chasm within which the city was built. The city was absolutely massive, having been built miles both outward and downward, creating an impressive architectural masterpiece.

"Whoa," is the only thing Kataal and Dahlik could utter upon seeing the great city stretch before them. The city was dark, and only the light from millions of those crystal lanterns provided light in the chasm. It was clear that this section of the chasm was more than a cavern deep beneath the desert.

"Bastion always did have a flare for the dramatic and overpreparing—build it massive or not at all, I guess," Xaddjyk said, looking out over the city.

"Why do you do that?" Kataal asked." You speak about Bastion almost like you knew him."

"Or something," Xaddjyk said simply. Kataal looked confused, but Xaddjyk walked away before he could ask anything else. Kataal looked over to Kara, and she shrugged and followed Xaddjyk into the next corridor. Kara described the city pretty accurately, but it's difficult for me to remember everything she said exactly. She says she has a perfect memory, but I do not. According to her she traveled through a lot of corridors, which got narrower and narrower as they got deeper into the city. It was clear architecturally that these corridors were not like the corridors in the upper city. The corridors in the city above were far wider than these, suggesting they were intended for significant traffic, as needed by a highly populated city. These within the undercity, as Xaddjyk called it, were narrower and fortified. They must have been built to prevent or impede any assaulting forces attempting to gain access to whatever lay beyond. As a further attempt to stop intruders, a massive door was sealed to block the path further down the corridor. The door was extensive and had no apparent means with which to open it. The door was solid stone reinforced with the same golden steel that the machines were made from. There was a single circular hole in the middle of the door, surrounded by a raised diamond-shaped metal piece. Inspection of the hole proved it to be a strange form of keyhole that required an unusual circular key with many flanges.

"Well, this is inconvenient. Is there any way around this door?" Kataal asked, examining the door and walls for a means to open it.

"I don't think this door is going to open. It's likely been sealed for the last couple centuries. Guess this trip is a bust," Dahlik said.

"Keep that positive attitude up, why don't you?" Xaddjyk jested as he pulled the staff off his back. Everyone watched him closely as he messed with the staff and checked the keyhole.

"I don't think that staff is the right size. It seems too big, and it lacks the obvious flanges, unless you plan to magically blow the door open," Dahlik said in a sarcastic tone. Xaddjyk looked over at him and shook his head as he flipped the staff upside down. He placed the headpiece on the ground while he examined the base of the staff. The staff was clearly too wide to fit into the keyhole, but this didn't seem to deter him any. Xaddjyk wrapped his hand around the bottom of the base and, through bouts of twisting and smashing, accomplished nothing at first. He finally twisted and pulled hard enough to rip what looked like a cap off the bottom, revealing a keylike flanged base to the staff. He threw the cap aside and gave Dahlik a stupid look and flipped the staff over. He fondled the headpiece, which was a central purple crystal mounted into the top of the staff. There were three rounded bars that came from the shaft of the staff up to above the crystal, connecting to the others by a round ring. The ring was slightly above the crystal, and the ring and bars were not connected to the crystal at all. There was a second ring that rounded the crystal slightly below the crystal's middle and connected the bars. Below the crystal the headpiece extended six inches down as a wider piece. The staff's headpiece was of the same golden metal as the city's machinery. The headpiece below the crystal was unusual and slightly flanged like the base of the staff. He grabbed the crystal with three fingers and twisted it slightly, which revealed a gear in the top of the headpiece. With his thumb he wound the gear until three long bars extended from the headpiece. Apparently the flanges on the headpiece were bars held down by an internal mechanism, and now six bars were extending from the top of the headpiece below the crystal. The top three were shorter than the lower three, and they were in line with the bars around the crystal. The two sections of bars extended from a single long flange and were connected with a pivot at the top and bottom of the lower headpiece. Xaddjyk twisted the top set of bars with his index finger a full turn counterclockwise before it would turn no more. The bars spun like a wheel spinning, all three of the upper bars and the upper half of the lower headpiece independently of the lower half and other three bars. After they spun a full turn, three additional bars snapped up in line with the upper two sections, extending the longest of the bars.

Xaddjyk lifted the staff and locked the key part into the keyhole on the floor in front of the door that mirrored the keyhole on the door. There were designs on the staff that obviously indicated how to use it.

After the key of the staff was placed, the others could see that he was murmuring something to himself. He then turned the longest bars clockwise, something like five-eighths of a full turn, before he stopped. It didn't seem to lock; he just knew when to stop like a combination lock. He proceeded to twist the second set one and a half turns in a counterclockwise direction before stopping. He then turned the last set four and two-third turns in a clockwise direction, and a sound could be heard within the door. The sound was like a churning of powerful gears that, after a minute, clicked the door's lock; and the door swung open like a double door, revealing more corridors. As the door swung open the lock released the staff, and Xaddjyk closed the three sets of bars on the headpiece. They locked into place with a click, and he put the staff back on his back.

"Oh, that's how it's a key—I was wondering about that," Kara said, looking at the bottom of the staff.

"Yep, Bastion had a fascination with combination locks and gear-work technology. This staff was made by him and given to Emperor Kadyuus as a gift. He gave it to him because he knew the emperor had no talent for magic and that the staff would never be used. However, as it belonged to an emperor, it would be very safe if he ever needed it," Xaddjyk explained as he started down the new corridor. The corridor went on for about fifty feet before it opened into a massive room, which the torch could not even partially illuminate. There was a set of stairs that led down to the floor of the room. They headed straight from the stairs until they reached a raised dais. Here Xaddjyk climbed up and placed the staff into a key port in the floor. He didn't wind the combination bars on the headpiece; he simply placed the staff onto the floor. Once he did, bright spotlights lit up from the ceiling along the walls and along a walkway that led into the distance. The walkway started some thirty feet from the dais, roughly the distance from the dais to the stairs they arrived from. After the thirty feet, the floor gave way to a pool of water on either side of the raised walkway. The walkway went for a good distance illuminated by the lights from the ceiling, offering enough light to see the scale of the room. The floors and walls of the room had gears built into them as well as other signs of Bastion's machines. At the end of the walkway, up two separate, small stairs, was a pedestal that held a large hammer.

"That's it. That's what you are after? A hammer of some kind?" Kataal asked rhetorically, squinting to see it properly from such a distance.

"It must be valuable for someone to have hidden it so far down here," Dahlik said with a kind of greedy look in his eye. Xaddjyk led the others along the walkway, but he did so slowly, erring on the side of caution. When they finally reached the end of the walkway and stood just below the pedestal that held the hammer, he stopped and seemed to have no intention to continue. I suppose he was waiting, and as it was, he didn't have to wait long. Dahlik the greedy bastard clearly came along for the treasure, not the guiding, and had his eye on the hammer. He pulled out a crossbow and jumped in front of the others with a threatening posture toward the others.

"Halt, I don' think so. This is my prize, but I do owe you thanks for helping me find something of great value. I must admit I was expecting gold or jewels, not whatever this is," Dahlik gloated eagerly with his crossbow trained on Xaddjyk and the others.

"Dahlik, what the hell are you doing You don't even know what this thing is or what it does," Kataal pleaded, stepping forward, slightly gaining the aim of Dahlik's crossbow.

"Perhaps not, Kataal, but I can imagine that if it's this ancient and possibly powerful, that several people of great wealth would gladly pay an exuberant amount to find out."

Xaddjyk rolled his eyes and shook his head slightly and said, "By all means, but I wouldn't." Dahlik stepped down for a second to stand at Xaddjyk's level, putting his crossbow in Xaddjyk's chest.

"Is that so? Well, I don't care. This wealth is mine." Xaddjyk shrugged and crossed his arms and had a slight smile. Dahlik approached the hammer with his crossbow in his right hand; he reached for the hammer with his left. He was slightly cautious and reached slowly. There was a mirror or some kind of reflective metal under the hammer that reflected the light from the ceiling upward around the hammer. As soon as Dahlik's hand broke the reflection from the mirror, a bolt of lightning struck him from above and sent him burning and flying to the left of the walkway where he, screaming, landed in the water.

"Uh-huh," Xaddjyk murmured, wiping a small chunk of burning Dahlik from his cloak. He approached the pedestal, kicking ash from the walkway.

"You knew that was going to happen, didn't you?" Kataal asked, following right behind him.

"Like I said, he always had a flare for the dramatic. How could he resist booby traps? I led us around or disabled several dozen on our way here." Xaddjyk walked past the pedestal, ignoring it entirely. He walked to the far corner of the walkway where a large anvil was located. The anvil was dusty and looked as though it hadn't been used in a very long time, even before this place was sealed up. Xaddjyk reached down and scooped a handful of ash that was accumulated around the base of the anvil. He threw the ash into the air, toward the fire, and it burst into flames, sparking in his hands.

"Fire and ash, blood of the forge," Xaddjyk said, dusting the anvil off as embers of the ash fell slowly onto it. Once the embers hit the anvil, strange runes began to glow red hot, and Xaddjyk picked up a dust-old hammer that was located not far away on a rack. He picked one hammer among a selection of several dozen and smashed the hammer onto the anvil as though he was forging something. Powerful red sparks shot from the impact, and he proceeded to hammer eight more times until the anvil itself glowed a powerful red with heat. He returned the hammer to its rack and turned toward the pedestal, grabbing a handful of the ash he had poured over the anvil and had just hammered into red hot embers. He approached the pedestal, blowing the glowing embers onto it, which brought something alive within. The hammer that was located on the pedestal began to open up with each corner sliding outward and the hammer that was mounted on it descending into the floor. Another more elegant hammer descended from the ceiling, where the light was emanating, floating within the light. Xaddjyk reached for it, allowing the rest of the embers to fall into the floor where the pedestal had opened up. As his hand touched it, an electrical surge emanated from his gauntlet to the hammer. After the surge, the glyphs on the hammer started to glow, and faint sounds started from within the city. He pulled the hammer from its cradle within the light, and the sounds became louder and louder. The sounds were of the machines coming back to life. The crystal lanterns went from a faint blue light to a blinding white light providing an amazing amount of light. The entire room was lit as though it was open to the sun and sky, and they could see the machines moving and returning to life. The great gears again turned, and the pumps and pistons cranked one more. The silence of the city was replaced by a roar of mechanical life churning and pumping. They left the walkway back, returning to the dais where they left the staff. After

Xaddjyk removed it, the great lights from the ceiling died, as they were no longer needed. Only moments after he placed the staff back on his back did a group of the corsairs enter from the stairs. They had removed their desert cloaks and revealed their golden armor and red silk garments. They were led by a white-clad woman who did not appear to be one of the corsairs. Her armor was pure white and appeared almost like Xaddjyk's in the strange and unusual shape of the armor. Her armor was far more feminine but was as complete and mysterious as his. Her armor had the same maddening angles and intricate engravings. Her armor was the opposite of Xaddjyk's but perhaps its equal. From their description and other things, it was as if his armor was built for war and hers more for defense and design. Xaddjyk walked down to meet them almost as if he knew her.

"Katalyna, I should have known," Xaddjyk said, resting the hammer over his shoulder.

"I'm not here for you. I need Bastion's Legacy, and you are the only one he told how and where he hid them," Katalyna said.

"And what? Are you going to take it from me, Katalyna? We have walked this road before, and never does it end in your favor."

"Things are different now, Xaddjyk, and I will now allow you to take the Hammer from me. Surrender it or your companions will suffer." The corsairs behind her pulled their crossbows and shot toward each of them. Xaddjyk didn't bother moving as the bolt shattered on his armor harmlessly. Kara swatted away the bolt intended for her, but Kataal was less skilled and was killed by it.

"Katalyna, I actually like him, you know."

"Who is this, Xaddjyk? I kinda like her. It's hard to find a woman of power in these days." Katalyna drew her sword, and all four of her corsairs followed suit. Kara had her spear ready, but it turned out to be unnecessary. Xaddjyk took a leap toward Katalyna, and once landing on the ground, he swung Bastion's Hammer, sending her flying in and through a wall to his left. The shock wave from him hitting her caused the corsairs to, well, explode into bloodied bits. Katalyna's impact with the wall was fairly spectacular, sending her straight through the cavern wall.

"Let's go. We have somewhere to be," Xaddjyk said, resting the Hammer back over his shoulder and heading back up the stairs. He made it about halfway up before he stopped and turned around, looking toward Kataal's body. He headed back down and went to Kataal, and with the Hammer, he struck the body. But instead of crushing the body, the Hammer glowed, and his body became covered by a clear crystal, like a diamond. After his body was fully encased, Xaddjyk pushed it to the water and stopped at the edge.

"Val Kaliuus Mal'Jjain Aada Sjjaii Jyyrkanu Taaysium Kataal," Xaddjyk said in some unknown tongue. I asked Kara what it was. She said it was an ancient prayer said upon the passing of warriors who died on the field of battle and that it was a great honor. He then proceeded to push his body into the water. As his body and his crystal coffin sunk, Xaddjyk, with a wave of his hand, set the waters on fire and then turned and left up the stairs.

"Who was that, Xaddjyk?" Kara asked, walking up to him.

"An old acquaintance. We go way back, and we have been on both sides of the 'friend or foe' fence. The last time we parted it was more the foe side. I'm guessing that the next time will be equally awkward," Xaddjyk answered without stopping.

"Next time? Isn't she dead?" Kara asked.

"Dead, no. She's hard to kill. We will be seeing her again, especially if we head for another of the Bastion Legacy."

"So if we head back it should take about three weeks," Kara said

"No, that's too long. The others could be in trouble. We need to get there quickly."

"Uh, you have an idea then? Bastion was a little before my time, so is there something here we can use?" At the top of the stairs Xaddjyk turned around, and looking at the pedestal that held the Hammer, he stopped.

"Bastion, you clever bastard,"

"Xaddjyk?"

"Bastion is using the power created in this place to power several things, including a Star Road."

"I've never heard of the Star Roads—what are they?" Kara asked as they stopped at the top of the stairs.

"Ancient magic that predates the Triaegis Empire; basically it's a means of travel. They are ancient roads that lead through other realms and allow rapid transit from any of the Archways to virtually anywhere regardless of distance. The Triaegis Empire gathered as many as they could but they could never replicate them or fix them when they broke. Bastion was one of the only experts on them; I'm guessing that he built this city partly to provide enough power to open one."

"Where is the Archway? This city is massive," Kara asked, looking around.

"It's here. I can feel it." Xaddjyk walked back down to the dais where the staff was to be placed. Upon closer inspection of the dais, and after piles of sand were dusted off, circular inscriptions could be seen around the keyhole. Xaddjyk nodded and replaced the staff into the floor of the dais. Once he did this, the ceiling lights again became active. He then opened the staff's winding bars the same way he did when he used it as the key to the door. He then wound the lower bars two and one quarter turns clockwise and then the second three and three quarters counterclockwise and the top and last set seven and a half turns clockwise. He was reading the directions from the floor of the dais. After he activated the staff's combination lock, the floor gears around the dais began to turn. At this point the entire dais began to lower into the floor. As the dais was about to lower below the floor of the room, Xaddjyk grabbed Kara by the top of her breastplate along the collar and pulled her onto the dais elevator. The dais lowered below the room after a hundred feet of solid stone until another room was exposed beneath it. This room was lit by similar crystal lanterns, but they were of different design and illuminated a purple light. They were not as bright as the fully powered crystal lanterns in the city, but they were clearly not the most prominent light source in the room. This room was in the opposite direction of the upper room. Obviously the pools in the upper room extended deep behind the wall of this room. Waterfalls along the back wall and both of the side walls poured into holes in the floor to somewhere below. At the end of the room, about the same distance as the walkway, was a massive Archway of light and energy.

There were massive gears and pistons on either side of the Archway that were tied to it by glowing rods that linked to its base. This room was clearly different architecturally than that of the city aside from the machines along the walls. The floor was decorated by depictions of lunar cycles and had unknown runes along with them. They walked along the room toward the Archway, taking time to examine the room. The Archway was composed of two large spiral half arches that rounded upward and came close but never actually connected. They were black and had glowing purple glyphs all along the spiral arches. There was a purple vortex inside the arches that became darker near the center of the vortex. The vortex spun around in a counterclockwise direction while the center spun in a clockwise direction. Dark purple flares swirled from the center of the vortex outward toward the outermost edges of the Archway. As he approached the Archway, Xaddjyk looked back at the dais where the staff was and he stretched out his hand. The staff was pulled from the dais and flew across the room and into Xaddjyk's hand. After the staff was removed from the dais, it began to ascend back toward the above room. He closed the bars on the headpiece and turned his attention back to the archway.

"This is the Star Roads?" Kara asked

"This is the Archway into the Star Roads. Come, you'll want to see this," Xaddjyk said with a smile as he passed into the vortex, disappearing. Kara followed without hesitating. The inside of the Star Roads was so amazing that I can barely describe it. There was no landmass or water or anything that resembled a place. The sky dominated the entire realm up, down, and everything around. There was a path made of pure energy, purple like the vortex and led around towards distant destinations. The paths were not straight and twisted and turned in all directions, forking and branching like a great tree. There were other Archways that must have been exits to other places. The sky was dark blue and had bright space clouds and brightly illuminated stars of all colors. These were not the most dominant features of this realm despite their amazing beauty. There were two massive moons that dominated the sky, one on either side of the path. The moon on the left was larger and brighter than the one on the right.

"Maphala and Yilum, the guardians of the Star Roads. Maphala is the largest and is the mother of the Stars. Yilum is the smaller and is companion of the travelers. They are ancient goddesses of the civilization that built these roads," Xaddjyk said as he walked along the path. The paths were fairly large, and there was no danger of falling off.

"This place is the most incredible thing I have seen," Kara said in awe and amazement.

"You can see why the Triaegis Empire sought this place so intently." Xaddjyk reached out toward the smaller moon, Yilum, and the whole realm blurred into a great purple light from Yilum; and suddenly they were at the camp where we stayed that night outside of Kan'Varil . . .

CHAPTER 5

BELATED VICTORIES

After we had been pushed into the darkness by the Clockwork Golem we wandered the halls of that endless labyrinth for longer than I could remember. All I can really recall is all the identical corridors filled with the same suffocating darkness turn after turn. I guess we knew that there was very little chance that we could ever make our way back to where the exit was. Even still, we were moving under the hope that the seal would be easier to open from within than it was on the surface, which makes sense if this was intended as an escape route. However, after so long in these corridors I don't think that the labyrinth was constructed to facilitate escape. Everything about this place suggested a much greater purpose something dark and mysterious. Why else would whoever built this place put such a powerful guardian to guard an exit when it could be protecting the place itself? This place was a tomb for whatever that thing was, and I don't think it was ever supposed to leave this place. Whoever built the golem wanted it to stay down here forgotten. The sounds of that infernal machine echoed throughout all the corridors, always reminding us what dangers awaited on the other side of this darkness. We walked around so many corridors that I think we were mostly just walking for the sake of walking since it was clear we were never going to get out of this maze on our own. I know I always wondered where Xaddjyk was, but eventually I just got too tired to even think about it. We were all starving and dehydrated as we had to ration what little supplies we had to make them last as long as possible. After all that time I could not tell the difference from one day and one year, so I could never say how long we were buried in that tomb.

Naturally we all got out of there at some point since I am writing this, and it's not just some dusty journal you found on my dried skeleton in the dark of the labyrinth. Xaddjyk and Kara did come for us after they returned from their desert adventure, and although we could not keep any kind of record of time, they sure did. According to Xaddjyk and Kara, they were gone for three weeks and four days. She kept very specific track of their schedule. According to her it took a day to get to Kal'Hinrathos and another in the city. It took five days to arrive at Kalamothae across the sea and a week and five days into the desert with the caravan. It took them another six days to find the city and sixteen hours in the exploration. They got to the camp around night on the twenty-fifth day. I can hardly believe that I was buried alive for almost a month though at the time it felt so much longer than that. By that point we had pretty much stopped walking and simply laid down in one of the unrecognizable tunnels waiting for a miracle. As you may have guessed that miracle did come, and in a strange way too. Apparently once Xaddjyk and Kara entered the labyrinth he used whatever magic was within the Hammer to awaken the powers forged into those cursed corridors. As soon as he brought the Hammer within the labyrinth's corridors, everything changed. A light began to glow through the darkness and everything came to life. The silt that had taken such a persistent hold of the walls began to crumble into dust. The corridors were illuminated by a golden light, and the corridors seemed to straighten before our eyes. As the darkness faded we found that just on the other side of the darkness ahead of us the entrance was waiting not but twenty feet in front of us. The rest of the survivors were lying in the corridor just behind us, and the labyrinth that had held us for so long changed into a straight hallway before us. Xaddjyk and Kara, having raised the darkness that was keeping us trapped down here, saw us all lying battered in the hall in front of them, and they rushed to see if we were alive.

"Hawk, what happened? Why are you down here?" Xaddjyk said, handing him another canteen that he had in his pack. He drank from it and managed to get himself up.

"We sure didn't have much of a choice. We encountered something in the great chamber before the exit," Hawk said, standing up and continuing to drink.

"Wait, what did you encounter?"

"I don't know, some kind of metal golem that burned with an internal fire. We encountered it in the great chamber, and the damn thing nearly killed us all," Hawk explained.

"And it attacked you?"

It was tossing people around the room. At least three people were melted by it."

"I don't understand. The Golems should not have been active. The Golems were built by Bastion, and like all his creations, they were all deactivated when he disappeared. I do not understand why this Golem would be active."

"You knew it was down here," Hawk said, handing the canteen to someone else.

"Yes, but it was supposed to be inactive, waiting for the Hammer's call. Something isn't right here," Xaddjyk said, looking into the distance. Now the hall from where we entered was straight, but as the hall headed further in, it divided into two forking paths.

"Xaddjyk, what the hell took you so long?" Kinterson said, handing back his canteen, which was empty. Xaddjyk tipped it over, and when nothing came out, he raised his eyebrow and looked at Kinterson, who shrugged.

Xaddjyk shook his head and started. "Well, blame Bastion for building his fortress way the hell in the middle of the desert. I got back as quickly as possible, but Day's End isn't what can be considered easily accessed," he replied, sounding almost sarcastic.

"Yeah, what good does it do us? We need to get the hell out of this tomb and try and find another way into the keep," one of the soldiers said.

"There is no other way. We have to go that way, straight through the gate and up into the keep, past the golem," Xaddjyk said, pointing further in.

"You have a plan then?" Kinterson asked with his usual tone.

"I have the Hammer. It should be able to take control of the Golem. We can then use it to assault the keep," Xaddjyk explained as he helped the other up.

"All right, everyone, we're moving out. Gather your stuff and let's move," Kinterson commanded, rallying the rest of the group. I was sticking close to Xaddjyk since he clearly knew where he was going and what he was doing. We started walking forward. The tunnels lacked the complex nature it had before. It was almost as if it was guiding us to where exactly we wanted to go. At some point the light from the great chamber became clear as well as two other groups, including Halkiir, who I hadn't seen for weeks, appeared before us. I was glad to see that he was alive, and I ran to greet them.

"Kya, you're alive! I wasn't sure if you had made it," Halkiir said as I hugged him.

"I agree. I saw so many die, and I hadn't seen you in weeks, and I was worried and wasn't sure if I would see you again," I rambled on before Halkiir stopped me.

"Xaddjyk," Halkiir said simply as he approached us.

"Halkiir, you look like hell, just so you know," Xaddjyk said, smiling and walking past him.

"So what's the plan? You got us all here again," one of the knights said, looking to Kinterson. Kinterson avoided the question, nodding his head to Xaddjyk while crossing his arms.

"We need the knights and the Sentinels for the assault on the keep, so I'll go in," Xaddjyk started before he was interrupted by Kara.

"You're not going without me," she said.

"Kara and I will go in and deal with the golem. You all stay here and wait for us to get this thing under control," Xaddjyk finished. Kinterson nodded in approval even though Xaddjyk clearly didn't need his approval. I had a front-row seat to what happened next. I pushed myself to the front of the group, standing in the doorway to the great chamber. The chamber was far brighter than the lights of our magical torches. I say *magical* because regardless of how long we were in the tunnels, the marvelous little bastards never burned out. Along the outer edges of the great chamber were deep trenches that I never noticed before due to low light the first time. Now these trenches were filled with glowing magma that illuminated the chamber. The magma flooded the chamber with red light and waves of heat. The center no longer had the pool and was replaced by a stone pad that glowed red hot and had the Clockwork Golem standing atop it. The chamber was far more lit than the first time we entered it and was actually well lit now. The golem was active and burned with the same red-hot steel. It was waiting like a guardian now awake. When Xaddjyk and Kara entered and approached, it did the same as before, greeting them with its loud roar and hot steam. The steam was useless against them, and they didn't bother trying to stop it. They were consumed in a thick blanket of steam that swirled around them. The golem seemed sure that he had killed them and waited as we did for the steam to dissipate. In only a moment, the steam began to swirl and thin as it was sucked into something. As it thinned, Xaddjyk and Kara became clear, still standing in the same place. Kara had her hand out, and a vortex in her palm was consuming all the steam. They both were wearing their helmets as if expecting that and were as always well prepared for battle. Now don't ask because I have no idea where they kept their helmets. They always just seem to materialize out of thin air. After the golem saw that they were unaffected and pretty well unimpressed, he again roared but did not bother spewing steam. Xaddjyk drew the Hammer, and the golem knew what they were planning and charged.

They both got out of the way in their own unique way. Xaddjyk used the Hammer, slamming it on the ground and riding the shock wave up and over the golem. Kara used her spear to push herself up and away from the charge. The golem was unable to stop and smashed into the wall. Once behind it, they saw something that clearly didn't belong. The golem was purely made of the gold steel used by Bastion as well as the red glow of heat. However, in the back of the golem was a large red crystal that was forcibly impaled into the golem's central body. The crystal had an inner red glow. It was clearly not part of the golem and seemed to have been forcibly speared through its shell.

"What the hell is that?" Kara said, looking over to Xaddjyk. He tilted his head and shrugged.

"Let's break it," Xaddjyk said simply, brandishing the Hammer. The golem pulled himself from the wall and started swinging at them both, but he was so slow to them. He was ensuring to keep both of them in front of him, seemingly defending the crystal. They danced around him, trying to get behind for several minutes futilely.

"Kara, you have to shatter that thing, take the Hammer!" He threw the Hammer to Kara.

"Xaddjyk," Kara started but stopped before saying anything else. She had a look in her eye that said "be careful" and nodded to him.

"Xaddjyk, take this," she started again, this time throwing him her spear. He caught the spear and showed very clearly that he knew how to use it.

"Oh yeah," he said to himself, swinging her spear, attempting to get the Golem's attention. He then charged the golem as it too charged at him. The golem swung its massive arm at him, but again Xaddjyk was quick and nimble. As the golem swung, Xaddjyk jumped, using her spear and landing on his arm and jabbing at it near the head and neck, easily garnering its attention. The golem would not tolerate it and swung with his other arm. Xaddjyk jumped sideways, barely missing its massive fist and landing on the ground and stabbing upward in the socket of its arm. With each jab of her spear, a small blue shock wave exploded out like magic, clashing with magic between the two. The golem was obviously very unhappy and kicked out, sending Xaddjyk flying across the room into the wall. It was pretty much the very same thing that he did with the one called Katalyna with the Hammer. The golem used this moment, when Xaddjyk was unavailable to swing, at Kara, who was behind him. He was unable to hit her, but it did keep her away from the crystal. With one of his swings he almost got her, but she was able to block with the Hammer. The impact was clearly something a magical shock wave that flew outward. The golem stepped back, but again it would not stop the attack on her. Xaddjyk was just pulling himself from the wall when the shock wave from the Hammer sent him right back in. When Xaddjyk finally got himself from the wall, still holding her spear, he had to brush off stone dust. He charged behind the golem, and using her spear, he struck at the crystal creating a powerful shockwave sending him back but he was able to maintain control. Kara was also affected, but she was able to regain control. The golem reacted to the attack, throwing his arms up almost as if it was in pain. The golem quickly spun around and tried striking at Xaddjyk. He dodged its left arm and the right hit him, barely sending him spinning uncontrollably. He landed inevitably on his head but managed to flip himself back on his feet, shaking it off. The golem roared in anger, and Xaddjyk jumped up, stabbing the spear into the golem's eye. As he got the spear into the eye, it backed away, and Kara, using the Hammer, smashed down on the crystal. Another powerful shock wave swatted them both aside. Xaddjyk managed to grab the spear, pulling it out as he was thrown aside by the shock wave.

Kara was getting up, and Xaddjyk threw her spear, and she threw the Hammer back to him. The golem was clearly angered by the damage to the crystal. The crystal was cracked and red energy was leaking from it. However, despite the damage, it wasn't done yet. The golem swung back, ready to fight, and more frantically now. The golem seemed undamaged aside from the crystal but still wasn't acting the same as before. Now Kara drew his attention as Xaddjyk flanked him in an attempt to get at the crystal. However, the golem was watching for the Hammer now. It charged at Xaddjyk, but he stood his ground. Once the golem got in range, Xaddjyk ducked under the Golem's arm and swung the Hammer at its breastplate, which was actually fairly potent. The impact knocked it back, and Xaddjyk rolled under its legs and swung the Hammer around, shattering the crystal into millions of shards and releasing a cloud of red energy. After the energy had dissipated and Xaddjyk and Kara got up from having been knocked away, the golem was standing normally, waiting for something. Xaddjyk held the Hammer aloft, and the Golem, with its right arm, crossed its chest in obedience to the Hammer. Kara waved the others from the tunnels into the great chamber. Most of them were still nervous about the thing that was trying to kill them last time. I was not worried, Xaddjyk and Kara were certain that the situation was dealt with, and so was I.

"Xaddjyk, everything good now," Kinterson said, approaching the chamber.

"I was right. This thing was supposed to be inactive. That crystal was not a part of the original design and must have altered its function," Xaddjyk explained, picking up one of the shards and examining it.

"What about the assault into Kan'Varil?" Halkiir asked.

"That's the way straight up into the keep. With the golem out of the way, the path is open," Xaddjyk explained, pointing to the open end of the room at the far side. It was larger than the rest and looked to be large enough to allow the golem to pass.

"Kinterson, Kara and I will lead the way up into the keep. We will take the golem with us," Xaddjyk started. I was waving my hand, and I think I might have jumped a little too in order to get his attention.

"And Kya apparently. Kinterson, take the Sentinels when we get up to the top of the stairs. Head right along the keep's ramparts. Halkiir, head to the left and enter from the keep's inner basements and fight your way upward. We will take the golem straight through the enemy lines and suppress any reinforcements from flanking you."

"A sound military strategy, but what about the siege weapons?" Kinterson asked in an arrogant tone.

"They won't bother firing at the keep. Not only would they risk hitting their own people but we are too far inside the walls of the fortress to hit anything accurately," Xaddjyk explained, starting up the stairs. Kinterson gathered all the Sentinels, which luckily—most from his strike force—survived the attack from the golem. Halkiir had a fairly equal number of knights with him, including the Knight Captain who had apparently survived as well. I was following Xaddjyk just in front of the massive Golem that was following us. I had my two short swords out, and Kara had her spear, but Xaddjyk was apparently tired of using a tool as a weapon, regardless of its power. He tucked the Hammer into his pack that he wore at his waist, and he went for his own swords. He only drew one, leaving the other alone, possibly for when things got bad, which they tend to do. The stairs from the great chamber looked like the rest of the labyrinth. At the top of the stairs there was a massive stone door that sealed by magic, but Xaddjyk used the handy staff to open the combination lock on the door and allowed it to open. The door opened in a wedge fashion with the center lower wedge sinking into the floor, and the other two opened upward. With the path now open, the room outside the door was of a completely different architecture and was more like the designs of Kan'Varil. It was clear now that we had entered the escape route within the keep. I couldn't hear any fighting, but we were unsure how the defenders fared because they had been holding the walls for a long time. We weren't exactly sneaking around, as the golem was loud as it moved. The other two strike teams had already left. We climbed a lot of stairs before we saw the fork he spoke of. The left path headed upstairs, straight up and around a corner. The right path headed around a corner but only a few stairs, and it was clear it didn't go up very high. Our path led directly ahead and up various stairs into the keep proper. According to Xaddjyk, we should exit somewhere in the keep's courtyard, which was pretty much where we ended up. We exited into the main courtyard and right into a battlefield. Apparently the assaulting forces had managed to get into the courtyard of the keep through the main gate, which they were able to destroy with a cannon.

The defenders were still holding the high ground at the top of the stairs with shields and spears, holding the marauders at bay. It was an impressive defensive strategy, as every time the marauders pushed up they all got speared. From what I can tell, the defenders still held inner walls, but the enemy was attacking it relentlessly. If they were allowed to take the wall, the defender's strategy would no longer work. However, Kinterson and his men were arriving on the inner wall and were assisting the defenders. I only knew because I saw Sentinels on the battlements shooting down into the courtyard. Once we entered the courtyard, everyone moved out of the way and the Golem charged ahead, knocking an entire line of marauders into the air. Their battle against the golem went about the same as it did for us with all the flying and melting. It was pretty nice having this thing on our side for a change.

The defenders noticed us right away and welcomed our assistance. After the golem rushed in, causing a mess of trouble for the attackers, Xaddjyk and Kara both entered the battle. Xaddjyk had drawn his other sword so he could maximize his slaughter and was doing a good job slicing people apart. I decided to enter as well. With my two short swords, I moved in, doing a pretty good job. With my agility and dexterity as well as the overall lightness of my weapons, I was able to inflict a lot of damage while moving in and out of the fight. I would usually enter and parry with one of the swords, deflecting it and using the other to stab at something vital and pretty much keep stabbing until he stopped kicking. It didn't occur to me that I was basically mass murdering my way through a bunch of people until it was over. It didn't take long for the marauders to decide to ditch and run for it. By this point there was a mountain of bodies in the courtyard, and I was covered in blood, having killed several of their guys. Of course at this point I also realized how tired I was. The defenders were more than happy to let the attackers leave even though I doubt any of them got away. As soon as they broke from the battle and left through the gate, Halkiir and his men started pouring out of buildings outside the keep and swarmed the attackers as they fled. I didn't see the entire battle, as Halkiir's men were swarming all over the area, and most were out of sight. I could hear the battle echoing throughout the fortress, and Kinterson's men rushed out to aid in the cleanup. Kinterson and Halkiir both were here in the keep, planning to meet with the defenders. They were obviously glad that the siege was lifted but were still suspicious of us.

"Greetings, friends. I must admit we had given up hope of reinforcements a long time ago. We weren't expecting Sentinels or whatever that is," one of the defenders said, walking down from the stairs in front of the keep's main gate.

"That's, uh, complicated. We are cleaning up the rest of the attackers. Is there anything else that you need?" Kinterson asked.

"Not from me. Commander Danyk and Baron Kyal would like to see you. There is an issue that we could use your help with," the defender said, leading the way into the keep through the great gates. There were something like thirty defenders with tower shields and long spears guarding the top of the stairs. The door was locked tightly, but after we broke the marauder's line, the gate was opened and supplies were brought to the defenders on the line. It was clearly a well-rehearsed event by the efficiency it was carried out. There were heavy archers in the gate, probably making sure that the gate could be defended if anyone tried to attack while the gate was open. Once inside I could see that there were a lot of wounded scattered about on just about every surface. They were being tended to by nurses in an attempt to get them patched and back into the fight. The soldiers that were left inside the keep were far less impressive than the defenders on the line. Their armor was more like armor designed for city guardsmen, and most of them were fairly young and clearly inexperienced. The defenders on the line wore massive folded tritonite plate armor. The tritonite plate armor is among the strongest armor I know of. The armor they wore was full body, and their shields were tall and thick. It was not really a surprise that they were able to hold the upper ground for so long with this technological advantage.

I could hear a lot more people than I could see, so I'm guessing that the garrison of Kan'Varil had brought everyone from the surrounding area into the safety of the keep. The defender took us deep into the keep, past the great hall and down into the highly fortified bowels of the keep. It was disconcerting to be underground again, but I tried not to freak out too much. We traveled pretty deep into another great hall far below intended for sieges just like this. The soldiers here were far more formidable than those in the great hall above and were more like the defenders on the line. There was a strategy table in the middle of the hall that had a series of maps on it. There were several important-looking people around it probably trying to plan their next move. One of them was clearly a noble, probably the baron, as well as Commander Danyk. Our entrance did not go unnoticed, and the baron waved us over. The defender pointed us in and then returned upstairs, probably returning to the line.

"Greetings. I am Sentinel Commander Kinterson. This is Sentinel Captain Halkiir and Knight Captain Falk. We are here to assist," Kinterson said, introducing himself. The baron shook their hands and turned to Kara with a questioning look.

"Paladin Prelate Kara of the Imperial Justiciars," Kara said without offering her hand. The baron was taken aback by her extremely illustrious title.

"A Justicar here, I see," the baron said, then turning his eye to Xaddjyk. Xaddjyk raised his eyebrow but said nothing even when the baron turned his head slightly, obviously asking.

"And you are?" the baron asked. Instead of answering, Xaddjyk just walked away. The baron shrugged and moved on.

"We weren't expecting reinforcements, especially not Sentinels and Justiciars, but I am glad for the help either way. However, the situation is not yet resolved," the baron said.

"How so?" Halkiir asked.

"There are three situations that need attention before the siege will be truly broken," Commander Danyk started. "First the enemy encampments still threaten the fortress with large numbers of marauders. With our walls heavily damaged, we cannot prevent them from gaining entrance. Second, the enemy artillery emplacements that destroyed our walls are still a danger to the fortress or any offensive we muster against the encampments. Finally we have an issue of a more personal matter—a foreign noble was here at the fortress before moving on to Aaomysiir."

"A 'foreign noble,'" Kinterson repeated.

"Princess Yulkii Taa."

"Yulkii Taa—as in Emperor Ming Chae Taa of the Ming Taa Dynasty?" Kara asked, stepping forward.

"Yes, she was here on a diplomatic mission with fifteen of her samurai guardians. They stopped at Kan'Varil to avoid a storm before continuing on to the palace at Aaomysiir. Unfortunately the marauders attacked and her guards were killed during a surprise attack from the catacombs into the keep and she was captured," Commander Danyk explained.

"How long ago was that?" Xaddjyk asked, turning around and stepping toward the baron and the commander.

"A little over a week ago. We do believe that she is being held in an old fortress in the foothills in the north."

"I will deal with Princess Yulkii Taa, Kya will be required for this task," Xaddjyk said simply, having returned to his emotionless personality.

"Well, that sorts the third objective, but what of the other two?" the baron asked.

"I will lead the forces to assault the encampments. I will take all the Sentinels and any forces you can spare," Kinterson said.

"Then I guess I will lead the remains of the knights in order to take out the cannon emplacements, but I believe that additional forces may be required," Halkiir said.

"We don't have much, but we will send as many forces as we can spare to aid you, but we must maintain a garrison to prevent the fortress from falling," Baron Kyal said.

I wouldn't worry about that. I'm leaving the Golem here. It will defend the gate into the keep. You can send additional forces," Xaddjyk said, heading toward the stairs.

"That takes care of that, I guess. We will send as many forces as we can spare. Commander Danyk, go with Commander Kinterson and take the heavy centurions and gather in the woods south of the enemy encampments. Halkiir, take the knights we have left from the garrison and assault the cannon emplacements on the ridge to the north of the fortress. You will need to take out the cannons before Commander Kinterson and Commander Danyk can begin their assault on the camps," Baron Kyal explained, pointing to the map on the table. Everyone nodded and started out. Kinterson was gathering the centurions at the gate, getting them ready to move. His group was at least twice the size of Halkiir's group, and its members wore considerably more armor. They were taking longer to get ready, which was okay since they couldn't do anything until after Halkiir took out the cannons without risking being fired on while attacking the camps. Halkiir's group was smaller, and its members wore less armor, more along the lines of light and medium armored knights. I figure they preferred lighter troops in order to strike at the cannons quickly. Halkiir had already gathered his forces and departed for the ridge, taking Hawk with them. They needed time to go around the ridge line and attack the emplacements from behind or risk being fired at by them. Halkiir led about twenty of the knights he brought with him as well as another twenty-five Kan'Varil knights. It took most of the day trying to get around the ridge and climb up to the top. From the Baron's intelligence, they knew that there were three different emplacements along the ridge, each with several cannons aimed at the fortress. It was almost daybreak by time they got to an overlooking position near the camp.

"So what's the plan, Captain?" the Knight Captain asked, standing on the ridge looking over the first emplacement. There were seven cannons aimed over the plain toward the fortress. These were obviously the cannons that besieged the fortress during the attack. There was a fortified camp around the cannons with a wooden makeshift wall guarding it and two tall wooden watch towers with lookouts. It was clear that the lookouts were there to ensure no one snuck up on the camp. There were dozens of tents within the wall and soldiers all over the place. Counting the men, there must have been sixty or more.

We are outnumbered, and they have fortification. I'm not sure how we can manage to defeat them without taking too many casualties, making assaulting the other two be impossible," one of the knights said, examining the camp. Halkiir carefully inspected the camp, looking for anything that could be used to their advantage.

"The powder stores an entire tent full of explosive powder. If we were to hit that with a fire arrow, it could easily take out half the camp, and we could shoot the rest from here safely," Halkiir explained.

"Sounds good. I could easily get an arrow in there, and when it comes to marksmanship I'm always there," Hawk said, pulling his bow and a special red-tipped arrow.

"Everyone spread out and draw bows. Hawk, you mind taking out those sentries first?"

"No problem," Hawk said, standing up. With a solid motion, he killed the first and then the second before they could make a sound. He waited long enough for the two to turn around in the towers. The first was hit in back of the neck and died instantly. The second guard turned around and was greeted by an arrow through the chin, killing him instantly. Hawk ensured that they wouldn't fall over by nailing them to the wood of the tower. He then pulled the red-tipped arrow, which he had placed on the ground, and struck it against his knee, lighting it on fire. He then shot it straight into the powder tent, and what came next didn't take long. The tent firs caught fire and then outright exploded. Now naturally I wasn't there, but Halkiir described the concussion and the heat of the explosion to being similar to when we were being attacked by the cannons. There were people flying and people running around on fire and even some people jumping off the ridge to their death. This plan actually worked quite nicely, as almost everyone in the camp was affected. Those who weren't dead or on fire were trying to help those who were. Only about a third of the soldiers in the camp were still in combat shape, and that was easily remedied. Everyone joined Hawk and started raining arrows down on the camp, and the defenders were in no shape to respond. The battle, if it could be called that, lasted only a few minutes before everyone was dead or dying. Hawk was the first down the hill and started taking care of any survivors.

"Well, that was easy. Let's hope the other two go as well," Halkiir said as he walked into the camp. Most of the camp was on fire, including the wood wall. Two cannons had lost their rigs, but all the cannons seemed to be intact although no powder remained, and all the cannonballs could be found scattered all around the camp.

"What do we do about the cannons now?" asked Captain Vos, examining the integrity of one of the cannons that lost its rig.

"Leave them. When we clear up the other two emplacements and the encampments, maybe Kan'Varil can salvage them and use them as part of its defense," Halkiir said, standing at one of the further cannons.

"Smart."

"All right, let's move on. We have two more positions to clear out before Kinterson can move in," Halkiir said. They gathered whatever supplies weren't destroyed in the explosion and subsequent fire, which wasn't much. When they left, the place was still burning though most of the fire had burned out. The walk to the next site was less advantageous, as it lacked the cover the other camp had overlooking it. However, the sun had set, and they did have the cover of night on their side. The lights from their torches made the camp pretty easy to spot even from a distance. The second emplacement wasn't far away though far enough away that they didn't know what had occurred. The explosion was extremely loud and quite powerful, and so they must have heard it as well and likely seen the smoke. Once they got in range of the second emplacement, they could tell that it was a smaller camp with a similar defensive. The garrison of the camp was on alert and had patrols out around the entrance and along the wall.

"Well, that ruins a repeat attempt now, doesn't it?" Knight Captain Vos said. They were hiding in a trench along the southeastern edge of the wooden wall. The patrols were four three-man groups with torches walking along the wall ensuring that no one approached too close. In the dark the watch towers were useless, and Halkiir and his group couldn't even see the men in the towers.

"I think I got this. If you can figure out where the powder tent is, I can get this in there," Hawk said, holding up a tightly wrapped satchel obviously containing the black powder.

"If we can figure out where it is, and I can get this in there, we blow this place up just like the first, but we need to get to the wall," Hawk continued.

"And past the patrols," Halkiir finished. Hawk nodded and then looked back to all the patrols walking along the walls.

"All right. Hawk and I will get to the wall and try to see where the powder tent is. Keep an eye out for the patrol. I think I have a new idea," Halkiir said, starting into the darkness away from the ditch. Hawk was right behind him, but the two quickly disappeared. They waited for the patrol to pass back toward the gate and quickly moved in. Hawk peered into the hole between the different logs used for the wall. The camp was well lit, and they could see the powder tent in the center of the camp near the cannons. The tent was well protected, and the soldiers were burying the powder under the tent, likely as a precaution. It was unlikely that they knew exactly what happened with the other camp, but they did not intend to take any chances.

"That's what I thought they'd do. This is so perfect. We couldn't have planned this better, come on," Hawk said, slipping away from wall and back into the darkness. They managed to escape into the shadow just as the patrol was returning. They sulked back to the ditch where the others were waiting.

"So?" one of the knights asked.

"Hawk, you seem to have this plan," Halkiir redirected.

"All right, they are burying the powder under the tent to prevent it from catching fire. However, using the powder I have, I can blast the area inside the tent, which will expose the powder. The powder will be spread over an area, and the fire of the tent will light it. Not only will this have the explosive force like the first, but the sand and dust will make breathing difficult. Everyone who isn't dead is going to run right out that gate where we can shoot them or whatever," Hawk explained.

"Well, let's do it. Everyone spread out around the entrance and get ready," Halkiir ordered, heading into position himself. Hawk approached the wall, waiting for the patrol to come back. When they did, he quickly shot them before they could call out. Once he got into position, he used the torch and threw the satchel into the tent perfectly. After scoring it into the tent, he made a little score gesture, pulling his arrow and lighting it with the torch. The explosion was small but kicked up a lot of dust, and some of it was black, probably powder. The dirt prevented the fire from reaching the powder. He then shot his flaming arrow right into the tent shards on top of the now-exposed hole, and the whole camp erupted into a fireball like the first one. This time, however, it was more dust than fire but also a lot of people were still sent flying. Not many people were set on fire, but there was a lot of coughing and people running to get out of the dust cloud. Of course as soon as they got out of the gate they were ambushed by Halkiir and his men. Those who remained inside were taken out by Hawk, who was shooting through the wall. This camp was smaller—only four cannons and a garrison of thirty men, no more. This camp was located nearer the cliff, and when the explosion went off, two of the four cannons fell off the ridge line, clanking all the way down. It was too dark, and there was too much dust for any smoke to be visible in the third emplacement. The supplies looted here were more profitable, as the explosion was less intense. They gathered whatever they could and pressed to the next camp.

The third emplacement was far more fortified and was located on an overlook above the main encampments. This emplacement was inside a stone outpost and was heavily protected. They must have been using the old outpost here as a defensive position for the encampments as well as a warehouse for their cannons and all their excess powder and supplies. The plan that worked on the other two positions was obviously not going to work here because the powder was likely being stored in the undercroft.

"Yep, this is interesting," Halkiir said.

"Cannons?" Hawk said.

"Yep, cannons. Let's bring the two from the last emplacement here," Halkiir said, looking back.

"Wait, we destroyed all the powder when we destroyed the emplacements. The cannons are useless," the Knight Captain said.

"Let's hope that the last encampment decided to be smart and not bury all their powder in the same place. Look around for recent digging. If we are lucky, they had other stores," Hawk said.

"Good enough for me. We will bring the two cannons here and dig up any powder as well as gather all the ammunition we can find," the Knight Captain said, gathering his men and returning to the second emplacement. It took several hours to move the cannons into position and gather as much powder and ammunition that they could within range of the outpost.

"So let's do this. Does anyone know how to use one of these?" Halkiir asked, looking around.

"I do, actually, and it really isn't that complicated. Come, I will show you," Hawk stated while beginning to instruct the others in the use of cannons. It took some time to get the heavy cannons into place along with all the ammunition and whatever powder they managed to find.

It took at least an hour to get everyone familiar with loading and firing cannons, but by this time it was still dark, probably sometime around midnight. They were pretty inefficient as a cannon crew, but the outpost was really old, which was lucky, as they didn't have much powder. They started firing on the wall, causing a fair amount of damage in the initial bombardment. Alarm bells could be heard ringing throughout the outpost, and troops were attempting to get their own cannons into position. However, before they could set them up, the entire facing wall crumbled; and a fair amount of people as well as a couple cannons came crashing down, burying them. Two more shots from the cannons right into the outpost caused an incredible level of damage, collapsing most of the outpost.

"Let's move. Charge in!" Halkiir yelled, leading his forces into the ruins of the outpost's collapsed wall. The cannons didn't take care of everyone, as a significant number of marauders came charging out to meet the attackers. The marauders had a clear numerical advantage, but I'm sure that Halkiir and Hawk would even out those odds. The battle quickly became a chaotic melee with everyone swarming in and around each other. It must have been difficult to tell who was who in the dark despite the illumination from the crumbled outpost. Halkiir was doing fairly well using his shield as both a defensive and offensive advantage. The majority of the knights tried staying close to Halkiir while he rallied them into a cohesive fighting group. Hawk, on the other hand, was staying back and shooting at will as well as using his bow as a club for those that got too close. The battle lasted a fair while, and it was difficult to tell who was winning. The marauders kept sending out reinforcements while Halkiir's men were not so inexhaustible. After several minutes it became clear to Halkiir that he may have to call for a retreat. Luckily for them, the marauders had the same idea and tried retreating. Of course that is just as bad, as they could not be allowed to return and tell of this before Kinterson could move into position. The marauders apparently had fewer men than they wanted Halkiir to think they did, and while chasing them down, they fell pretty fast. They eventually had no choice but to turn and fight again. The battle became another dusty melee, but this time Halkiir had the advantage. By time the battle was finally over the sun was starting to rise, and Halkiir and had lost over a quarter of his men in the battle. After their victory they headed to the outpost in order to send the signal to Kinterson so that they could begin the attack.

"So we send the signal then we join the battle, right?" the Knight Captain asked as they climbed the ruined wall. Halkiir looked around once they made it up to the top of the outpost, where they had their cannons set up.

"Or not," he said with an unusual tone.

"What? Are we just going to leave the battle to Kinterson?" the Knight Captain asked, following him up.

"We are down almost half our men, and the rest are exhausted and haven't eaten or slept since midday yesterday. They simply aren't ready for another prolonged conflict. They'd be more a danger to Kinterson's men," Halkiir said, looking down to his men. His men were resting on whatever they could and had broken out rations and were eating and drinking whatever they had available.

"However, they do have some experience using these, and these will be very useful, don't you agree?" Halkiir asked, smiling and looking to the cannons.

"Oh, how perfect, use their own cannons against them. I really have no problems with this strategy," Hawk said, laughing while he picked his gun.

"All right, men, gather supplies and grab a cannon. It's time to repurpose some iron," Halkiir finished, grabbing his own cannon. The men at the bottom grabbed as much powder as they could from the undercroft and gathered the ammunition from the back. The piled as much as they could and then loaded their cannons and waited for Halkiir's word.

It was cannon fire that got Kinterson's attention. Kinterson got a look at the ridge and saw the cannons firing on their own camp.

"Gather up. It's time," Kinterson said, smiling and rushing back down to meet his men who were waiting in the woods not far from the camps.

"What's going on? What's with the cannon fire?" Commander Danyk asked, following Kinterson to the front of the force.

"Halkiir must have decided to repurpose them, another advantage for us, and I'll take it. Listen up! Avoid the northern camp. Now let's move," Kinterson said, leading the charge himself. The marauders in the camp were already rushing around due to the cannon fire, and many were seeking escape in the woods. When Kinterson's men rushed out, they were forced to assemble a line in order to defend against Kinterson's charge. All the marauders that could gather together pressed against the assaulting forces. Kinterson's men were more organized and smashed into the first wave of marauders, cutting them down. The centurions were doing pretty well at keeping their momentum, and unlike Halkiir's force, they remained together, preventing the marauders from dividing them. After their charge was finally slowed, they had to round together while the marauders attacked from three sides, trying to collapse the centurion line. The centurions held their line against the marauders, but they couldn't move from their position. Halkiir was still bombing the northern camp and had moved to hitting the incoming marauder forces in an attempt to ease the pressure on Kinterson. There was only one cannon that was targeting close to the centurions while the other bombed randomly around the camps. Kinterson had a few close calls, including a cannonball that ricocheted off the ground and flew right over his head, making a whining sound as it passed. Kinterson ducked it but it was close. The battle was going fairly well despite appearances to the contrary. The marauders assaulted against the centurions for, at the very least, several hours, outnumbering them extensively. The centurions had such an advantage in experience and equipment that the additional number just meant more for the slaughter. I can see how this type of assault would have been impossible with the cannons, but now the differences between the two forces were clear.

The centurions took only mild casualties, as the marauders were never able to amass a proper response while the cannon bombardment continued. The marauders eventually gave up and broke their attack trying to get away. Kinterson ordered his men to chase them down, and for the first time the centurions broke rank and separated. The battle was already over, and Halkiir had already stopped the cannons while the centurions hunted down the stragglers.

"Commander Kinterson, the remaining marauders are fleeing into the woods. I've ordered the centurions back—no need for them to try chasing them down," Commander Danyk said.

"Good, our part is done. Now the rest is up to Xaddjyk, Kara, and Kya . . ."

CHAPTER 6

YULKII TAA

A round the time that Halkiir was getting ready to leave, so were we. Now we would have left around the same time, except that, unlike him, we only had three people to gather supplies. While Halkiir was readying his people, we were already prepared and on our way out. Xaddjyk and Kara had restocked their supplies and dropped the excess that were required for the desert but not needed for the temperate environment of this region of Kaladiin'Aaiyyr. Now I doubt I explained exactly how they carried their supplies with their armor, so I'll go into details here. They wore packs on their lower backs hooked to their belts. There were two sets of packs, one on either side behind their legs. Each set had two individual packs that were separate, one above the other. They were worn by a leather strap over the shoulder across the chest and back. As such, the packs in the right side were strung over the left shoulder and the opposite for the left packs. Now there seemed to be standardization with these packs since every time I saw them they all seemed similar. These packs, at least for Xaddjyk and Kara, appeared to be designed for the armor and had the same color scheme and designs as the armor it was made for. Xaddjyk's packs were black and had the silver stitching, making it clearly his. They appeared to be leather or leatherlike material.

The upper-right pack, the smallest pack he had, was mounted between the belts across his chest to the belt on his waist and was about seven inches long and six inches wide. The upper packs on both sides overlapped the lower ones while the lower packs were larger. The right pack was small and had the main pouch as well as two smaller pockets on the outside. This pack was filled with Xaddjyk's navigation supplies, including a compass, a sexton, and his magical map. He also kept a black leather-bound journal and smaller logbook as well as his pen and a well-sealed inkwell. He kept other nonconsumable supplies in there, some of which I could not describe or explain. The lower pack on the right side was bound to his waist belt and was secured tightly around his thigh and fifteen inches long and the same six inches wide. Now in the desert, he used this pack to carry his extra water supplies. Here he removed the water satchel and was currently holding the Hammer in there. The Hammer was a good fit, and the shaft of the Hammer stuck out about half an inch from the top of the pack. This pack had about twelve smaller pouches on its outside, which had long cylindrical vials with unknown liquids in them. On the left side his upper pack was larger than the one on the right, being about ten inches long and the standard six inches wide. This pack contained all of his food supplies wrapped inside, whatever they were. There was also a small canteen hooked to the outside of the pack. The lower pack was the same size as the one on the right and contained his extra water pouch. In the desert it was necessary to have two extra pouches, but here one was good enough. There were also two large pockets, one just below the bottom of the upper pack and one below the upper pocket. The pockets looked filled, but I have no idea what was in them. Each of the packs was carefully and tightly secured to the armor so that they couldn't move. He also had a large canteen secured on his belt in between the two sets of packs on his back.

Kara's packs were pretty much exactly the same aside for being white with purple stiches to offset the black of her plate armor. Her packs were similar in size and purpose. Me, however, I only had two packs; and they were small. They were so small that I could barely fit the journal within which I wrote about these exploits.

Well, anyways, back to the story at hand. As soon as we, mostly them, refilled their supplies, we all headed out. We moved out before Halkiir could gather his men though we had to travel farther than he did. We had to travel far to the north, at least two days' worth. The travel was boring and the sights all the same. I swear I have never seen so many trees in my life, and they are everywhere. I thought it was odd that the marauders would have a base so far away from their encampment. According to Kara, this was an old keep made a long time ago in order to defend a road that hasn't been used in over a century or two. The keep was abandoned sometime after the road became useless and has been occupied by numerous bandits, thugs, raiders, and gangs of all types since. Kara was under the impression that the marauders attacking Kan'Varil likely sold her to whomever currently runs the show here, likely slavers or someone wanting to return her for ransom. The route to the keep led us through a long forest and into a ravine with a river. We followed the river for a while before the ravine turned away, and then we walked along a vacant and vast plain. We camped on the plain the first night before continuing on into another forested area for a while and then along a ridge line following another river. We eventually turned off, heading northward into a very hilly region, which was actually annoying especially when it started raining. We camped under a stone overhang to get out of the rain for the second night before continuing the next morning. Of course it was still raining, but we pressed on regardless into a semi foothill region where the keep lay beyond. We had to climb up a layer of cliffs into a rocky area that overlooked a lush lowland where an ancient highway once snaked through The road was barely visible, having been overgrown. There was a small stone castle in the distance, which even from a distance looked in rough state.

"There it is, Kan'Nuumak, one of the oldest remaining outpost in this region," Xaddjyk said as we looked from high on the cliff some twenty or thirty miles from the keep. Now for clarification the term *Kan* is short for Kanculius, which means castle. Also when I call it a keep, it's because the castle walls around the keep have long since eroded away, leaving only pieces and rubble. The keep walls were mostly intact, however, still making the outpost pretty defensible. The fortress had a similar layout, but the architecture was primitive in comparison. This analysis was made possible due to a spyglass that Xaddjyk had with him. He had since removed the wrapping from when he was in the desert, and it revealed more of the spyglass. The spyglass was golden metal that looked exactly like Bastion's machines and must have been another of his inventions. Unlike typical spyglasses, this one had several knobs and gears on the top of the spyglass intended to focus the inner lenses. The knobs and gears were connected to the inner lenses. There were four sets of knobs, so clearly four lenses. Each lens had one knob on top to change its horizontal angle as well as one on the right side for the vertical angle. The gear on top was to change the rotation of the lens, likely for magnification. The spyglass was fifteen inches long and, unlike its counterparts, could not collapse due to the knobs. He kept this spyglass in a long, rectangular pouch mounted vertically on his side, right next to his right side packs.

"Too far to tell any specifics. We better be cautious on the approach," Xaddjyk said, putting his spyglass away.

"We can likely get a better view of troops around the keep from hills just west of the wall," Kara said, standing up and starting down the side of the cliff. From the bottom of the cliff we had to hack our way through thick overgrowth as we walked through the low forest around the old road. We were avoiding the road because despite it being overgrown, it was still fairly open and possibly patrolled. It was slow going, and it took us all day to get to the area near the hill. There was barely enough light to get any kind of view of the keep, but Xaddjyk managed to anyway. However, something he saw clearly confused him, as he had a double look.

"Problem?" Kara asked.

"There is about a hundred men down there, but they aren't marauders—they're samurai," Xaddjyk said, confused and looking through the spyglass again.

"Samurai? This far from the Chae Empire?" Kara remarked, looking at Xaddjyk.

"Maybe she isn't in danger after all. Maybe she was rescued by her own people after she was captured. The baron said she came with a group of samurai. These could be her people," I so intuitively added, feeling clever. I had never heard of the Chae Empire, but I have seen people who wore clothing like theirs and had strange eyes. I guess they came to Kal'Hinrathos for trade like everyone else.

"No, wrong banner. Any rescue would have been samurai from the house of Taa. These look like they are from the house of Nagisumka or perhaps Zhu, or Tasaki," Xaddjyk explained, putting his spyglass away.

"So, hundreds of samurai—that's not good odds, Xaddjyk, not even for us," Kara said.

"Yeah," Xaddjyk started, standing up. "There is a back way through a tunnel over there." He walked down the hill and into foliage, and we followed him in. We walked for about an hour until we found a hole in the ground with a ladder leading straight down. The cover had long since been destroyed or lost, and the hole was just open. Xaddjyk was the first in ignoring the ladder and just jumping in, followed by Kara who also just jumped in. I decided to be smart and not do that and use the ladder. I got about halfway down when the ladder buckled due to age and I fell. Luckily, Xaddjyk was there, and he caught me before I could hit the ground. He wasn't surprised and put me down before heading into the darkness. We lacked a torch, and so Xaddjyk resorted to another means of illumination. He unbuttoned one of the pockets on his lower left pack and pulled out a handful of small, spherical objects. He cast them into the darkness, making a lot of rattling and bouncing, followed by sounds of them rolling. It was only a few seconds before they started to glow with a clean blue light, providing a good level of illumination. He then proceeded to pull out a small clawlike bracelet that was made of platinum and gold and was decorated with gems. It was only as big as my wrist, and the claws didn't look very big either. It looked like it was intended to snap around someone's arm instead of being slipped on. Xaddjyk approached me and grabbed my right hand and placed the bracelet on my wrist, snapping the claws shut around my arm. He wasn't forceful, and the bracelet didn't hurt or anything, but it was cold and weird. As soon as he put the bracelet on me, all the small orbs started rolling toward me. They kept a reasonable distance, but they were responding to the bracelet. I have never seen anything like it, and it didn't look like Triaegis magic, so I have no idea where he got it.

"Okay, let's move," Xaddjyk said, walking further into the tunnels. Kara and I followed, and as I walked, the glowing spheres followed me, ensuring that the tunnels around us remained well lit a good distance in front and behind us. They made a metallic sound as they rolled with us, not quite loud enough to echo but definitely enough to prevent a stealth assault. We walked for quite a while down crumbling tunnels before we arrived in a large underground structure that contained several rooms. The underground complex looked military, we entered into an ancient barracks with dozens of tattered beds stacked two by two along the walls. We wandered around the complex, which revealed itself as part of the fortress, probably a garrison housing safely underground to protect it from siege weapons. There was a desolate armory and a forge with adequate ventilation. The whole chamber was in a fair amount of ruin, but the structure was mostly intact.

"We will spend the night here—it's safe and we can keep an eye on the forces above. With luck, these tunnels will lead us into the keep, essentially bypassing the army above us," Xaddjyk explained, standing at the forge.

"What if they move her in the night?" I asked, switching gazes between the two of them.

"Not likely. Their camp wasn't packed, and they showed no signs of preparing to leave. They were also securing the woods around the keep. They have no plan to leave anytime soon," Kara explained, picking out a nice spot for her to meditate. Typically when I slept, Kara sat cross-legged and looked almost like she was mourning, but that doesn't make sense. Xaddjyk usually roamed or joined Kara, but this time he had a better idea. He was at the forge's anvil and swept two centuries' worth of dust and rubble off the anvil. He spent several moments checking the integrity, and once he was satisfied, he pulled out the Hammer, placing it on the anvil. He started pulling large chunks of rusted metal coated in dust and ash from the forge, clearing it. Once he was satisfied that the forge was cleaned out, he grabbed the Hammer and stood with one foot on the edge of the forge, leaning in and striking at the inside of the forge three times. Each strike cast up magical sparks, and upon the third strike the forge became engulfed in fire. This was not natural fire and was blue and gave off so much heat I had to move farther away to avoid being melted. Kara was smart and her spot was in the armory. Most of the dividing walls had crumbled, and only the major load-bearing walls remained. Xaddjyk returned to the anvil with the Hammer and started pounding on the anvil. The magical sparks started flying, and it looked like he was forging except that he had no raw materials. As he hammered away on the anvil, something started appearing as though the Hammer was creating the material from nothing. It took him about five minutes to finish what he was making, which was a long pair of tongs that looked like they were made of a blackened version of the gold metal used by Bastion. He slid the tongs over and started hammering again, making something else. With each heavy stroke, he followed with a quick, lighter one. After forging for twenty or so minutes, he picked up the tongs with his left arm and was using them to move whatever he was creating around so he could keep whichever part he was currently working on in the center of the anvil.

I must have watched him Hammer for hours or something before I got bored and fell asleep. I was so tired that it was no surprise that I fell asleep regardless of the loud hammering. I must have slept for six or so hours, and when I woke up he was already done making whatever he was making. The Hammer and his tongs were sitting on the anvil, but there was no trace of what he made.

"Hey, catch," Kara yelled, throwing me a bundle containing a portion of dried meat and a chunk of bread, typical in the field meal. Xaddjyk appeared from one of the rear rooms with a handful of some leather that I couldn't quite make out.

"Try these—they should prove better than your current armor and quite a bit less conspicuous," Xaddjyk explained, placing it on a table next to me. I went to see what he was talking about. Upon investigation I found that he had made a set of leather armor with a long white outer cloak. Now it was complicated to figure out how to put it on, but luckily Kara offered to help. The armor consisted of a set of fine, rich-brown leather with golden threading. Though he had made me a new pair of boots, they looked almost exactly the same as the ones he gave me before, aside from it being a richer color and stronger design. The armor was pretty similar to the boots as each individual piece was secured tightly with straps. The boots were of a rich brown and went as high as my thigh and had belts all the way up to ensure the boots remained tight. They had a strong leather design and a rugged sole intended for use in harsh environment. The sole had several sections, where the standard leather sole was replaced by steel and had strong steel teeth designed for gripping or climbing. The toe was narrow and also had metal teeth intended for climbing rock surfaces or perhaps buildings. There was a long knife strapped on the outside of the right boot down below the knee under the belts intended to tighten the boot. The boots were worn over a pair of strong but tight cloth pants that were tight in order to allow the boots to be worn over them. The pants were white and soft as silk and yet felt strong and resilient. There was a tight undershirt with long sleeves that hugged the body well. Over the shirt there was a leather vest that strapped around the waist and chest as well as a piece that was strapped under the crotch to ensure that the vest didn't slide upward. The vest was worn like a corset, being pretty tight around the chest and secured by three sturdy belts. It also contained a number of pockets and pouches as well as slots for knives. The vest didn't cover the arms so the armor had long leather sleeves that went up to the elbow. They looked just like the boots and had belts all along them, securing them tightly. They had holes in the end to allow the four main fingers of the hand through as well as another for the thumb, securing it in place around the hand. The leather sleeve covered the palm of the hand with a tough leather pad that was high friction, further proving that the armor was intended for climbing.

The final piece of the armor was a white cloak that was worn under the leather vest around the chest but extended down to my legs. The cloak around the chest area was pretty simple since it was meant to be worn under the vest. There no point in wasting time with any details no one would see. The back of the cloak exited under where the vest ended with a single triangular piece down to about my thigh, just above where my boots ended. Beneath that triangular layer there was a second layer that extended down to below my knees. Now the first layer was a solid triangle with an angle of about ninety degrees. The second extended far below it and was a far more of an acute triangle, getting thinner the further down it went, meeting at a pretty sharp angle at the bottom. There was a nearly identical triangle on the front that extended downward to just above the knees. The triangles were lined with purple, which followed the triangles all the way up and under the vest. Though the cloak had no sleeves, it did have strong shoulder pieces that wrapped around the upper arm, further securing it in place. The cloak was worn like a shirt and was loose everywhere, except around the chest and waist where it fit tightly for the vest. It had a large hood with the same purple designs that looked equally useful for keeping dry and hiding one's face. The armor also came with a complete set of packs that conformed to the standard, like Xaddjyk's and Kara's, which attached to the belt and the vest.

"How does it fit?" Xaddjyk asked, returning to get the Hammer and the tongs, which he placed in the rear pack where the Hammer typically went.

"Uh, it's kinda tight and heavier than my old suit," I said honestly. The armor was so tight that it made breathing fairly hard, but I'm not sure if it was because it was tight or because I wasn't used to it.

"Good, you'll get used to it, and it won't seem so tight. Now let's move. It should be around morning topside—and don't forget you kit," Xaddjyk said, pointing to my leather-bound thief's kit. This armor had an intuitive hook and pouch made especially for it. Now my kit was a long leather roll that, once unrolled, was about forty inches long and nine inches wide. The kit had various pockets and hooks that held my tension wrenches and various lock picks and skeleton keys. I also had a wax mold box and several small vials of wax for making wax copies of people's keys. I had magnesium ribbons for situations that require an incendiary solution. There were several small brushes, a magnifying glass, a small hammer and chisel, several sticks of both charcoal and chalk, and a vial of potent acid. Finally there was a pair of narrow-nosed pliers, two small knives, and a bar cutter for bolt locks. The whole kit rolled up to a bundle and had a strap that secured it closed. It took me several years to buy, borrow, or steal everything in my kit, and I have used everything in there at some point. It was a pretty nice burglar kit, and it has served me well.

After we gathered everything, leaving my old clothing there on the table, we headed deeper into the tunnels. That night I had removed that weird bracelet thing but put it back on as we left to get those weird spheres to follow again. The bracelet was a hard fit with the leather sleeve, but the sleeve was tight enough that it still fit. We walked through a series of tunnels that connected to other small complexes and barracks that must have webbed all around the area under the old fortress. Many of the passages had long ago collapsed under the weight of the earth above them, but we were still hoping that one of these passages led into the keep. We had to keep redirecting due to dead ends and hope we were heading in the right direction. We reached another dead end, but this one was different. This dead end was a solid wall, not a collapsed tunnel. Xaddjyk kept walking toward the dead end as if he knew something we didn't. Once he reached the wall he started feeling around the walls beside the dead-end wall. After a short time he found a small hole and, inside, a lever. I know he found a lever because once he pulled it, he actually pulled the whole thing out. The lever must have broken a long time ago and was clearly useless. He drew the Hammer and struck the hole where the lever used to be. He then used the top of the Hammer to push the wall open, like a hinged door. This opened up into a large, open room with a stairwell at the far end and decayed weapon racks everywhere else. This was clearly an armory and seemed to be well stocked with a wide variety of weapons. However, all the weapons here were ancient and decayed over centuries of sitting unused. There were tall stone stairs in the distance that led up presumably into the keep proper.

"Hold up. This leads into the keep, and I doubt that this will remain unguarded for long," Xaddjyk said, taking the bracelet off of me and placing it back into his pack. He kneeled over with his palm open, and all the spheres gathered together, and he quickly collected them, placing them in with the bracelet. After he gathered them he started up the stairs slowly and carefully. We were clearly deep underground, as we had to go up three floors before we saw the first enemy soldier. Xaddjyk was crouched at the top of the stairs, peering over along the floor and remaining as unseen as possible. I was standing behind him and was able to see over the top of the stairs. There were two samurai guarding a corridor that led to the next set of stairs as well as a corridor that forked off, leading deeper into the keep basement.

"Two guards," Kara said, stepping behind me so she could also see.

"Hmm, five," Xaddjyk corrected, and though we couldn't see the other three, we just took his word for it.

"Kara, we need to take these out as quickly—no retreat. We cannot allow them to inform their friends," Xaddjyk continued. Kara nodded and readied her spear, but due to the close quarters her spear was more a liability than an asset. However, she apparently had a solution. The spear stood about six foot four, which was taller than her even in the heeled boots she wore. This made a useless weapon inside, but its designers had clearly accounted for every possibility, including this. She unlatched several hooks on the headpiece, removing the entire headpiece except for the spear tip itself and one of the side blades, placing the headpiece into her lower right pack. She extended the edged blade outward into a claw hook. She then twisted the lower shaft about four feet and pulled it off. This revealed a two-and-a-half-foot-long blade, turning her long spear into a devastating close-quarters weapon. The new weapon was a short spear about four feet from the tip of the half-foot-long spear, head to the end of the two-foot-long sword. This short spear was usable with one hand or two.

"Kya, remain here," Xaddjyk said, getting up.

"Xaddjyk, I have combat experience. I can back you up," I argued though now I see how stupid it was.

"Listen, Kya, these people are out of your league. I've seen you in battle—you are brawler, which means you rely on instinct and reflex, not training or experience. This isn't a bad thing, and one day you will end up being a skilled warrior. However, these men have been trained since they were old enough to hold a sword. They have been trained and honed into more than just soldiers—they are weapons. Their instincts and reflects are a result of decades of repetition and training and make up the most skilled military forces in the world," Xaddjyk explained, looking to me as I nodded in understanding. Xaddjyk nodded and moved up the stairs, and Kara was right behind him.

"Hey!" Xaddjyk yelled at the two samurai who drew their swords and started yelling in an unknown language. Kara rushed past Xaddjyk, catching one of the samurai off guard and got him in a weapon lock. The two of them were engaged in combat, and I could see exactly what Xaddjyk meant by "well trained." The samurai was able to keep up with Kara, and she was one of the greatest warriors I have ever seen. She was using both ends of her short spear, spinning it as she fought, showing extreme skill and dexterity. Xaddjyk was his usual self, not using a weapon and attempting to get the weapon from the samurai who was really reluctant to lose his weapon. They used their *katana* with two hands and used them with much skill and speed. The samurai that attacked Xaddjyk made a mistake and swung too strong and missed, which Xaddjyk took advantage of. He dodged the attack and drew the samurai's *wakizashi,* or his smaller secondary weapon. The wakizashi, like the katana, was held in his sash blade up, so he was able to cut the samurai as he drew it. The samurai reacted well, pulling his katana in preparation to fight an opponent armed with a similar weapon. The samurai struck at Xaddjyk, stepping into the strike for more power, and he deflected the blow with his forearm, using it like a sword redirecting the blow down and away and then jabbing up with the wakizashi through his underarm. Xaddjyk left the wakizashi in the samurai, grabbing for the katana instead.

While Xaddjyk was fighting with the second samurai, Kara was actively engaging the first. She had the advantage of a more versatile weapon, having a double-edged spear, the claw hook, and a double-edged long blade. It was this versatility that led to her victory. She was able to parry every attack that he swung with the blade, and she was able to force him into overextending himself by grabbing his katana with her claw hook and pulling him away. She then sliced his hands, forcing him to drop his blade, and impaled him through the chest.

"Kya, catch," Xaddjyk said, throwing a crossbow and a small quiver filled with bolts strapped to it. I caught it and was able to examine it nicely. The crossbow was pretty short, as if designed for me or someone small like me. The body of the crossbow was made completely out of metal, and yet it was fairly light regardless and had a well-formed stock and trigger guard. The metal was golden steel, like that used by Bastion for his technology, but was blackened like when Xaddjyk used the Hammer to forge the tongs. I guess he had forged this after he forged my new armor. Many of the features were made of a black metal, which complemented the golden steel well. The upper wench bar was connected to an intricate clockwork mechanism on the side and within, possibly designed to maximize the tension of the bolt while making it easy to draw. The bolts had several different tips designed for different situations. The tips were black metal, but the shafts were of the blackened gold metal like the crossbow. The fletching was made of golden feathers, and the rope of the crossbow was a golden thread, making the crossbow quite ornate. The details of the crossbow were complicated due mostly to the complex gear work on both sides. Despite being an amalgamation of Bastion's golden steel and blackened steel, it was extremely light and well balanced.

"A crossbow?" I asked, securing the quiver safely on my lower back.

"It keeps you out of sword range, which might not be a bad thing," Xaddjyk said, and I nodded smiling. The moment was short-lived, as the other three samurai Xaddjyk mentioned were just around the corner at the end of the corridor and were aware of us. They charge forward down the corridor, and Kara was prepared with her short spear and Xaddjyk with his stolen katana. Xaddjyk ducked the first one and engaged the second one while the first samurai was starting to turn around. Kara engaged the one Xaddjyk ducked while the third got pushed out of the corridor and started toward me. I had loaded the bolt onto the rail hook and cranked back the wench bar, which locked it back into place. The wench was pretty easy to pull even though the rope was at a high tension. The samurai had to dodge Kara, who was swinging her short spear at his head. He was forced to engage her before she reengaged the other samurai she was fighting before. The one that was coming to me turned back to me, and I pulled the trigger on the crossbow, and the recoil was impressive and startling. While I was startled by the recoil, I didn't realize until moments later that the bolt had pierced through the samurai's throat and he chocked and bled to death slowly. It was horrible and accidental. Xaddjyk and Kara were fighting with the other two in a tight corridor, and the tightness ended up being an advantage. I'm not sure how, but they seemed to know what the other was going to do almost as if they were reading each other's mind. Kara turned around quickly, stabbing the samurai that Xaddjyk was fighting in the back while Xaddjyk stabbed the one Kara had been engaging in the head. Xaddjyk dropped the katana and started down the corridor as if seeing why they were guarding it.

Around the corner there were several large open rooms filled with large boxes that contained a jade dragon on their sides. I guess the samurai and whatever lord controlled them had brought these supplies with them, and from the amount they had stockpiled, they could stay here for months.

"Xaddjyk, you seem to know this place. Where is the dungeon from here?" Kara asked, standing behind him.

"The escape route here ensured no dungeon could be built here. The keep's dungeon is in the next structure connected to this one via a tunnel one floor up. After that the dungeon should be two floors down. There are several gates and strong doors between here and there. Hopefully time has taken its toll on them," Xaddjyk said, heading back to the samurai bodies.

"Kara, grab a leg and drop them in one of these rooms," Xaddjyk said, grabbing the legs of both the samurai and dragging them around the corner. Kara, smiling, headed into the first room where the other three were and grabbed two more, dragging them back was well. I figured it was up to me to finish up, so I tried getting the other, the one I killed accidently. He was heavy, and I had to use both hands to move him. I got to about the corner when Xaddjyk appeared, grabbing him by the top and bottom of his chest plate and picking him up. He carried him to the nearest room and threw him in. He actually threw him pretty far, which I suppose would make the expression "I trust you as far as I can throw you" rather inaccurate. He threw him in the room without regard for either the man or the crates, shattering many of them with his body. Xaddjyk, at the last room, used his Gauntlet to throw a large fireball inside, setting it ablaze. He did this for the other four rooms, effectively destroying all of their supplies. We got out of the corridor quickly and started up the stairs before the smoke alerted others.

"That smoke should draw a number of the samurai from their posts. We just need to wait." Xaddjyk said, moving into a dark room across the corridor that led to the next structure. After a few minutes the smoke from below was flowing upward into both the corridor and up the stairs into the keep hall. Samurai from both the other structure and the keep hall came rushing down to the fire, trying to save their supplies. With the confusion and hiding in the smoke, we slipped through the corridor and to the next structure. We were following Xaddjyk and were trying to be careful and quiet as to not sound an alarm among whoever was left on guard.

"If they are holding her in the dungeon, it'll be in the deepest two or three levels down, and you can expect several samurai guarding every floor between here and there," Xaddjyk said, peering around the corner to where the stairs were. There was a single samurai guarding the top of the stairs.

"Kya, give me that thing," Xaddjyk said, holding his hand out to me. I gave him the crossbow loaded with a bolt, as I figured that is what he wanted. With one hand he leaned out and shot the samurai right in the head. He let out a muffled gurgle as he was nailed to the wall. He handed the crossbow back and moved into the room. Kara checked the body, and Xaddjyk secured the corridors around the room. I looked down the stairs and saw no less than ten highly decorated samurai, each wearing horned helmets and scary-looking face masks. They stood as stoic as statues, not caring one bit about the fire. Xaddjyk pulled me away from the stairs and peeked down there himself.

"You stay here, Kara. We got ten elites in the next room and possibly more below. You are going to need the shard for this one," Xaddjyk said.

"I have this crossbow—I can help," I protested, reloading the crossbow with one of the bolts that, I think, was intended for armor piercing.

"You are—make sure that no one comes from upstairs or from down there. No one can be allowed to inform the others," he continued. I crouched down by the stairs in preparation while Xaddjyk and Kara started downstairs. Xaddjyk drew both his swords, which was a good sign that the situation was bad. Kara was going with her short spear but also drew her short sword. Now I didn't see the battle, but after much pressing, Kara finally told me about it.

So here it is—sorry but this is really complicated, so try to bear with me. Once they got down the stairs the ten elites were waiting around them in a half circle, weapons still undrawn. They were clearly looking for an honorable fight, which is what I have come to expect from them. Xaddjyk's swords were pretty large as far as swords go and were, like Kara's spear, too long, given the circumstances. Also like Kara, his weapon was designed with adaptability in mind. Now his blade started out larger at the hilt and got thinner along the blade and got larger near the tip of the blade for obvious reasons. The blades slid seamlessly into the larger section near the cross guard. The longer middle piece of the blade was greatly shortened as it slid into the lower section. The blade was shortened considerably and went from thirty inches to about twenty-four inches. Now six inches may not seem like a lot, but with swords six inches is the difference between two-handed and one-handed. He held his right blade normally and his left blade in the opposite direction. Kara held her short spear with her right hand at the center of the staff and wielded her short sword of twenty inches with her off hand.

The ten elites all drew their swords with one motion and in sync with the others. The battle started with two of the elites from either end attacking at Xaddjyk and Kara with two each. They seemed to respect the honor of duels but knew that the odds were not favorable. They clearly held their duty to protect this room over personal honor. They were far more skilled than the others we faced earlier and even armed with two weapons. They focused most of their attention on the defensive. Unsatisfied with their progress, the leader ordered more in. Now I'm going to describe Kara's actions first. Now of the ten, Kara was able to kill four and Xaddjyk the other six. Kara was defending against the attacks of the two that were accosting her originally when the two more moved in. This was clearly what she was waiting for because only then did she start fighting. First she waited for them to surround her, and then she ducked down, swinging her spear in a circle and forcing all the elites back off in order to defend themselves. With their swords up defending against her spear, she drove her sword upward through the chest of the first elite. She left the blade in him and then, using her spear with both hands, pushed the other three back off her, giving her room. She was incredibly strong, being able to push three of them back at once. This gave her time to draw her sword out of the dead elite. Now this happened so fast that after she impaled the elite and pushed the others back, she was able to draw her blade out of the dead one before he fell to the ground. The other three charged in, and she blocked the strikes of two with her spear and, with her left hand, called forth a powerful wave of force, sending the third flying back into a wall.

After blocking the two they were forced to back up in order to regain their balance before striking again. The first moved in, followed by the second shorty after to avoid hitting each other. She grabbed the first's blade, using a small slit on the hook, which was designed as a sword breaker. She deflected the second man with her sword by swinging as hard as she could, causing him to become unbalanced. She threw her sword down, forcing it into the stone like when you throw your knife into the dirt so it sticks out. She grabbed her spear and forced it in a weird direction, actually breaking his katana, which surprised everyone, including Kara. This elite was well trained and quickly went for his wakizashi. She would have gutted him there, but they drew their weapons very fast, and as they are blade up he can use it lethally on the draw. She had to back off or be sliced as he drew his weapon, and there was the other two who were returning. She was surrounded again, but this is where she liked to be. She drew her sword out of the floor in preparation.

They started striking at her from all sides, and she seemed doomed. She was dodging in a circular motion before she decided to strike low and stabbed the third elite in the foot with the blade on the bottom of her spear. He reacted to the pain very well, but he couldn't resist it entirely. After she spun around again, she decided to strike him again, this time through his knee with the same blade. Once she pulled the blade out he dropped to his knee, and she was able to push the other two away. She swung around again and decapitated him with her short sword. The other two flanked her on two sides in order to attempt to gain an advantage. She attempted to assault the first when the second stabbed her from behind. The blade missed the center of the body and pierced through the chain mail and her side, near her stomach. When he pulled out the blade, more damage was done, as she was pulled along with it before falling. The first elite tried to stab downward in order to finish her off, but she rolled out of the way. She struck upward and through the first elite's side but was unable to retrieve her spear after the strike. The second was quick to reciprocate and stab at her again. She couldn't move out of the way fast enough and was pierced again, this time under her chest plate and into the vital region it protected. The samurai tried to pull his sword out, but she grabbed the blade with her left hand, preventing him from taking it. With her right Gauntlet she, while screaming, sent out a powerful burst that caused the elite samurai to explode into a red mist, sending parts of him flying in every direction. The poor bastard screamed before he died like he knew what was coming. She just lay on the floor wounded and bleeding all over the place.

Now at the same time Xaddjyk was engaging his own problems. His weapons and armor were clearly more advanced than theirs. and they knew it. They were trying to use superior numbers to offset the disadvantage they had. Where four went after Kara, the other six, including the leader, went for Xaddjyk. Five of the six were attacking him from every side, but he didn't seem fazed by it. His attacks were so powerful that when he landed blows he'd send them stumbling backward. He was able to strike two, even three at a time, and they were incapable of breaking his defense. Finally he got tired of playing around and outright kicked one of the elites to the ground, and he impaled another elite through the chest with his right sword, nailing him to the wall behind. That guy didn't die right away but spent his last few moments trying to get the sword out of himself. It was clearly pinned deep enough in the stone wall that he wasn't able to budge it. He lashed out, switching his left sword to his right hand, slashing with a flurry of strikes and forcing three to withdraw. The fourth moved in to aid his fellows but failed to do so. He struck out, and Xaddjyk blocked with his sword and grabbed the elite's wakizashi out of his sash in the direction he was originally holding his left-handed sword. He jabbed downward with the wakizashi through the samurai's throat. The leader was tired of watching his men die and drew his *dai katana*, which was basically a really long katana. This was about the time that Kara was first injured; and Xaddjyk, though he didn't acknowledge it, knew. He drew his sword out of the wall where he left it and switched his swords to their appropriate hands.

Now in case you're lost, there are three left including the leader. The leader was waiting in the background, awaiting an opportunity to move in himself. His sword was longer than most, and he needed a good amount room to use it. His fellows were moving around, trying not to get hit by Xaddjyk. While taking a short break while the two samurais were waiting for an opportunity to strike a critical attack, Xaddjyk figured it was time for a change in strategy. He returned his left sword to its scabbard on his back and instead armed himself with the Hammer. I guess he thought that despite the fact it wasn't a weapon, it was funny. The second samurai struck out and was blocked by Xaddjyk's sword, and he used the Hammer to shatter his sword. Now this did not surprise me, as from what I've seen, the Hammer is very powerful. The shock wave resulting from the Hammer's blow sent the samurai who just lost his sword to fall backward on the ground. Xaddjyk swung the sword and the Hammer at the last elite, sending him backward where he then went to the one still on the ground. He dropped the Hammer on his chest, breaking his ribs. He then drew his left sword and impaled him with it, picking the Hammer up again. The second samurai started toward him, but Xaddjyk was more interested in the leader. He threw the Hammer at the second elite, sending him flying and splattering into a wall. Xaddjyk with his right sword only decided to finally deal with the leader. He decided to return his sword to its normal size to engage the leader's dai katana.

The next sword fight was pretty impressive while the two of them went at it. The leader was a well-trained swordsman and was doing well as the two of them clashed blade. Though Xaddjyk's sword was shorter and more maneuverable than the dai katana, the leader was using a variety of techniques to adapt. Usually a katana is used with two hands on the hilt, but he was less concerned about technique. He used his sword with two hands on the hilt or one hand on the hilt and the other on the blade, or just one hand on the hilt and the other out away from his body for balance, whatever he thought was useful at the time. Xaddjyk had the advantage at short range, but the leader's longer sword gave him an advantage at a distance. Both of them landed good blows, but neither of them showed any injury. Finally after several minutes of tense battle, Xaddjyk grew tired of the confrontation and decided to deal with it. The leader swung his sword down, intending to hew Xaddjyk in two. Xaddjyk grabbed the blade, stopping it in his hand. Xaddjyk began to blaze with internal fire. He clenched his teeth and the fire grew. The left gauntlet with, which he had grabbed the leader's sword, was engulfed in fire and sparks, and drops of liquid fire poured from his hand. The blade glowed red, and the heat flowed in waves from the steel. Xaddjyk thrust his sword into the floor, and his right gauntlet became engulfed in the flame, same as that of the left. A small river of liquid fire was flowing before his feet as it dripped and poured from his hands. The leader pulled his wakizashi while keeping his right hand on his katana. He tried to strike out, but Xaddjyk's left hand blazed as bright as the sun and forced the leader to look away. The leader swung his wakizashi, and Xaddjyk caught it with his other hand, and the fire exploded onto the leader. He caught fire and burned alive inside his armor, screaming. It was a less-than-merciful death, and as he did it, Xaddjyk turned almost evil. The swords he was holding melted in his hands as the leader burned and died. After he killed the leader, the fire burning from him flowed out, and he returned to his normal self as though he was possessed by a demon or evil spirit that manifested fire with in him.

Kara was wounded not far away, still bleeding away, and Xaddjyk went to her aid. They didn't say anything while he checked her wounds. He cupped his hands together like when you pick up water. His hands were empty, but he acted like it already had water in it. The silver etchings along his gauntlets and up his armor began to glow with a bright white light. The space in his hand glowed pure white, and when the light subsided his hands were filled with pure water. He spaced his fingers slightly so the water began to drip out over her armor and her wound. Once all the water was gone he stood up and Kara appeared to be okay. He offered her his hand and helped her to her feet.

"You okay?" he asked, handing her her spear, which was still buried in a guy's side, and sword, which she took. The sword she returned to its scabbard, and her spear she took in hand.

"I'm fine, thank you. That's the third time I needed her tears," Kara said, dusting herself off. He nodded, returning to the samurai leader, and started to rummage through his gear until he found a large rusted key.

"Kya," Xaddjyk called up the stairs, and I came running down hoping no one saw me.

"Hey, how did everything—whoa, what happened?" I asked after seeing all the bodies scattered around in varying levels of dismemberment. Xaddjyk noticed that there was a table along one of the walls near the stairs. He approached it because of what was on it. The table had two swords of highly ornate and decorative design. The scabbards and hilts were purple with highly intricate golden designs. They were clearly of a higher level of craftsmanship than the other weapons that I have seen these samurais use. There were also other items as well, including a large silk robe and sash with the same color scheme. There was a collection of high-quality equipment and clothing accessories. There was also a set of packs following the same standardization as the rest of us but with the purple-gold color. Xaddjyk started putting everything on the table into the packs as if he was planning to bring them along. After he had gathered a large collection of princesslike accessories, both clothing and equipment in nature, he grabbed the four packs and the two swords.

"Kara, Kya," he said, getting our attention. After we both looked over to him he threw Kara the four packs, which she then proceeded to clip to her back. He then handed me the two swords without saying anything. He then headed for the stairs down carefully, ensuring there was no ambush.

"The lowest dungeon should be just below. I doubt they would have these ten here otherwise," Xaddjyk explained, heading down into the next room. The room below was darker and lit by only a few candles and showed little evidence of through traffic of late. Most of the cells were either open or destroyed by time and nature, but there was a single cell farthest from the stairs that was still mostly intact. The door was sealed, and there were several dozen small candles gathered on the floor in a circle around a shady individual. They were particularly crappy candles and gave off almost no light. Xaddjyk approached the gate with the key in hand, but as he got close he saw how damaged the gate was. He dropped the key and grabbed the gate and yanked it off its lock. The lock went flying off the bars and onto the floor, and the gate swung open freely. Xaddjyk stepped into the cell. The shady figure was sitting with her back to the cell door and looked back at Xaddjyk as he entered.

"Xaddjyk, I wasn't expecting to see you," the figure said in a female voice with a fairly strong accent. Her accent was not like the accent that Dus'Pois had but was more Oriental in nature.

"I came as soon as I heard. I surely wasn't expecting you so far from the empire," Xaddjyk said, still standing just inside the gate.

"Yes, well, things are hardly normal. It seems the entire world is falling into chaos and anarchy," she said, standing up. Xaddjyk stepped out of the cell and into the slightly more illuminated room. The woman followed him out, finally revealing herself in the light. She was taller than me but not as tall as Kara, standing at maybe five nine or ten. Kara was likely five ten herself, except that her boots were heeled and gave her two or three inches. The woman also wore boots, unlike the samurai who were wearing sandals. Her boots were not heeled and were flat bottomed. Her clothing was purple with the golden designs like the swords and clothing items we found upstairs.

"Has the chaos spread to the empire as well?" he asked.

"Yes, it first started with small raids,, and now some of the noble houses are getting restive against the empire. My father is pushing back against them, but without a shogun the military is divided," the woman said, answering his inquiry.

"What happened to the Lord Shogun Ilunaga?" Xaddjyk asked.

"Dead. He fell ill some time ago and died about four years hence," she answered.

"I see, Kara. Kya, this is Princess Yulkii Taa." Yulkii Taa bowed her head slightly in acknowledgment as did Kara and myself, seeing the others do it.

"Yulkii, there are a lot more of your 'friends' to go. You will need your armor," Xaddjyk said, pointing to an armor stand that held an exquisite suit of purple and gold samurai armor. This armor was different than that of the other samurais I have seen today and incorporated several advantages. Her armor seemed to be mostly samurai in design but had aspects taken from armors from other nations, including ours. Xaddjyk and Yulkii approached the stand where Xaddjyk pulled the Hammer out.

"Is that Bastion's Legacy Hammer? He told you where he hid it, didn't he? Did he tell you where he hid the rest of his Legacy?" she asked. Xaddjyk shrugged and smiled. He held the Hammer up, pointing it to her armor.

"Oh yes, please, always room for improvement," she said, backing up. He struck the armor so hard I'm surprised the armor didn't shatter. The hammer blow sent sparks of blue magic, and the armor started to glow with white light. After the white light subsided, her armor had changed both in color and in design. Her armor was now blackened slightly, and the material it was made of had changed. Typical samurai armor is made of strong steel and wood. The wood had morphed into a blackened steel that, texturewise, looked like the metals used by Bastion.

"Thank you, but do you mind helping me getting this on? It's complicated," she asked, looking between the armor and him. He sighed and started pulling the armor off the stand. She started with the boots and worked her way up, eventually getting to the chest plate and its various attachments, which is where Xaddjyk's help was needed. It only took about ten or so minutes to get her armor on with help.

"Yulkii, we have some of your things," Xaddjyk said, waving to us. She attached her various sashes and her swords and her packs. Her armor did not have a helmet or one of those masks, and her armor came with various belts that held her packs and her swords unlike the other samurai who do not use leather belts.

"We have an escape route secured that will lead us a fair distance out of the walls," Xaddjyk started as he began toward the stairs.

"Wait, we cannot leave. The situation here is more delicate than you know," she started.

"What are you talking about? Whose samurai are these?" he asked.

"Lord Zhu," she said as if it was no real surprise.

"Well, that makes things more . . . interesting. What is he hoping to accomplish by capturing you?" Xaddjyk asked.

She shook her head. "I don't know and that's the problem. Lord Zhu has always been a bit of a megalomaniac, and so I am surprised that he hasn't come down gloating about how he captured me and revealing his dastardly plan and whatever. His silence is actually extremely unnerving, and I have only seen him once, and that was when I first arrived."

"Then I guess we need to have a chat with him. We cannot allow him to continue whatever he is planning. Zhu is likely cooking up some kind of scheme to overthrow Emperor Ming Taa," Xaddjyk said. Yulkii was about to say something but simply nodded instead. As Yulkii gathered all her belongings, including her swords and armor, we were prepared to move on. We headed upstairs, trying to avoid further confrontations as we headed up into the keep proper. Unfortunately, in order to get into the keep proper, namely the great hall, we had to move back into the next structure and up into the keep. Now the smoke from the fire had started thinning, which suggested that either they got the fire under control or it died out on its own. This meant that all those samurai were likely returning to their posts or they were out searching for how the fire started in the first place. We got up to the stairs when Xaddjyk stopped Kara. He was noticing the holes in her armor made by their last battle.

"You need to expedite your armor's healing process," he said, examining the two holes.

"I've devoted as much of my concentration as I can muster into healing the armor. You mind?" Kara said, holding her right hand and Gauntlet out toward him. Xaddjyk took her hand with his own Gauntlet, and magic started glowing in between the two, and her armor began to repair itself quickly.

"Whoa! How . . .how did you do that?" I asked looking on in amazement. After a few moments her armor had been completely healed and looked as if it had never been damaged.

"Ancient magic. Her armor was constructed using similar means as the Gauntlets and, as such, has a magical essence of its own. The armor is capable of healing itself over time as well as the ability to adapt to various situations. Also, it is self-maintaining, ensuring that the armor stays at the pinnacle of perfect condition for as long as the magic remains within it," Yulkii Taa explained.

"Ancient magic?" I asked.

"I'm a bit of a scholar on ancient magic and technology from the Triaegis Empire and whatever bits remain from before that even."

"Come on, we need to deal with this before we are discovered here," Xaddjyk said, heading toward the corridor and heading to the next structure. We couldn't see anyone waiting in the room at the end of the corridor, and everything looked clear. We entered the room, and Xaddjyk looked down the stairs, seeing if there was anyone running around down there. I looked along with him but quickly pulled back because it was like an ant hole down there with dozens of them running around and standing about. A lot of them appeared to be sealing the door in front of the fire, which amazingly still persisted. The smoke was barely escaping through holes in the door, where they have yet to seal it with wet cloths.

"Well, that should keep them occupied for a while longer," Xaddjyk said, smiling and turning around. He peered up the stairs, looking for any surprises.

"Well we need to climb up three floors to get to ground level and another two to reach the upper keep," Xaddjyk said. We got up two levels before we had to hide while half a dozen retainers or soldiers who are not samurai, just random soldiers who serve the house, ran past. They were carrying buckets of water and long cloths to aid the others downstairs. Now they were clearly too concerned with getting their supplies where they were needed and weren't looking for us. We scurried up to the ground level and up to the level below the great hall before a detour was needed due to a large number of guards waiting below the stairs to the upper keep. Xaddjyk was leading us to a secret entrance that led through the rear behind the throne in the great hall. The halls of the keep were decayed and crumbling pretty bad. I highly doubt that this keep will last another hundred years, judging by the state of these halls. I was mostly just hoping that the route he was leading us to was still intact.

He led us around strange corridors and halls and around the center of the keep. This took longer to navigate but also kept us away from their patrols and holdings. Finally we managed to sneak our way to a hidden stairway located behind a bookshelf in one of the smaller libraries distant from any of the main hallways or important rooms, a good place for a secret escape route, I suppose. He pulled several rotted books off the shelves, which long ago became illegible and were soaked and stained. He seemed to have remembered which books to remove since they couldn't be read anymore. He pulled off eight books from the shelf and activated small buttons in the stone behind where the books were. There was a particular order to the books and buttons, and once he hit all eight, the book shelf and the stone wall behind it slid clumsily into the floor. Something must have been broken as the contraption did not go down all the way and still stuck out of the floor, so we had to step over it in order to get to the stairs. These stairs were tight and narrow and sharp as it headed up to the next level. There was a release lever at the end that opened a door to what looked like a war room. There were two doors at the other end that led into the throne room, but one of them was collapsed, obviously requiring us to use the other. As soon as we entered through the door, no longer worrying about sneaking, we entered the throne room, where several more of those elites were waiting as well as one highly decorated samurai. He was sitting cross-legged on the ground, facing us as if waiting.

"Ah, so it is. I thought I smelt the distinct odor sulfur. I did not account for your interference in this matter. I guess you have come to know why I am here, what my end goal is." The samurai started standing up. "Taa, I should have killed you when I had the chance, your cursed family has been nothing but a blight on us. Your family never deserved the throne in the first place. The events are already set into motion now, Taa, and not even your friend can stop the inevitable change in power. The empire will finally have an emperor worthy of the throne and a shogun to rally our armies."

"Nagirama, he's planning to help you get the throne and you make him lord shogun," Yulkii said with a voice of disbelief.

"Strong leadership is what the Chae Empire needs now, and I swear it will get it. Your father is already dead and nothing can stop it. I have always planned on killing you, but now your comrade will make that very difficult. We will see how many it takes to kill you, Xaddjyk. Kill them!" he finished, walking out of the great hall. All the men in the room drew their weapons, and the door was flooded with an army of samurai and soldiers rushing in preparing to attack.

"No!" Yulkii yelled, summoning a magical aura around herself. The magic was jade and were emanating from her hands, and she redirected it all to her right-handed Gauntlet and shot a beam of energy onto the ground in front of us, creating a strange portal. The portal looked like the Star Roads portal inside the Archway, but the vortex was jade. Xaddjyk knew what it was and stepped forward in the attempt to allow us time to get through. Kara grabbed me and pushed me and followed herself. I don't know what happened after I entered, but I do know that just before Kara pushed me in, Xaddjyk created a powerful wave of force, knocking everyone back and onto the ground. Shortly after Kara and I entered, Yulkii followed and Xaddjyk was right behind her. The portal closed behind Xaddjyk, and no one followed us in. Though the portal may have looked like the Archway, but this was not the Star Roads. The world was all green and flowed with strange waves of energy in various shades of green throughout. There were no moons in this realm, and there were no Archways in the distance. We stood on a single floating pedestal of energy suspended among the flows and currents of energy. We were in this realm for only a few minutes before it collapsed, and we appeared on the ridgeline overlooking the valley and the keep. It was clear that this was Triaegis magic based on the magic of the Star Roads but far less sophisticated. It could only take us a short distance from the point of origin as well as it being unstable. The realm that it passes through didn't have the moons or goddesses that the Star Roads had and thus didn't have whatever protection they offered.

"You have been studying the knowledge of the Triaegis Empire. I wonder what other powerful magic you know," Xaddjyk asked rhetorically, pulling out his compass to check for direction.

"Where to now?" I asked, stepping forward.

"We should return to Kan'Varil and meet up with the rest of our party. We should also not remain around here too long," Xaddjyk said, checking his compass and starting back toward the fortress. He turned around to look down toward the keep that we had just escaped from.

"Uh Xaddjyk, this is bad, right?" I asked, pointing down toward the road out of the keep where the army there was marching out. The army was a lot larger than we had thought, as there must have been three or four hundred samurai and soldiers. They were marching out the keep with their wagons and whatever supplies they had left.

"Yulkii, how exactly were you captured? Be specific," Xaddjyk asked, turning to her.

"Well, after we arrived at Kal'Hinrathos we headed to Aaomysiir. We stopped at Kan'Varil for the night, and in the morning the attack began. About two weeks into the siege the keep was assaulted from within by samurai loyal to Lord Zhu. Two spies loyal to Zhu within the keep apparently opened the escape route out of the keep and allowed them to enter. They clearly didn't want to take the keep like the marauders and instead just want to capture me. It was rather flattering, really," she explained specifically.

"That means that not only do they know where Kan'Varil is, they know their way around the keep too. It's very possible that they are returning in force to prevent us from getting word back to the Chae Empire. Kan'Varil is not in good shape anymore and cannot sustain another attack," Kara said.

"Who cares if they are heading there?" I said, and everyone looked at me strangely. "I mean there may be like couple hundred of them, but the fortress is still guarded by the Clockwork Golem. Won't they have about as much luck attacking him as we did the first time?" I explained, and everyone seemed less annoyed at me.

"She has a point. The golem will make assaults on the fortress extremely difficult," Kara said.

Xaddjyk shook his head. "That Golem is a centurion class, and though I doubt they can destroy it, it can only attack so many at a time while the rest just move around him."

"Wait excuse me, what is this about a Clockwork Golem," Yulkii asked interrupting between us.

"One of Bastion's Legions, a Steel Centurion to be precise," Xaddjyk explained in a hurry.

"Wow, really? I heard rumors about them but never have I found any evidence to suggest that they were ever built. None of the Golems were ever found nor is there any evidence of them," Yulkii said ecstatically.

"We have to get to the fortress before they can and warn the defenders that a samurai army is on its way.

"Xaddjyk, if that army gets there, Kan'Varil will fall. We need more than one Steel Centurion," Kara said, concerned.

"Perhaps, but I doubt it," Xaddjyk said, smiling and looking through his spyglass. "Take a look," he finished, handing the spyglass to Kara and then me. We were pointed on the other side of the cliffs in the lowlands where Kan'Varil was located. There was a massive dust storm a fair distance from us. It had to be an army since they were coming from the northeast along the road leading to Aaomysiir. It had to be knights finally coming to check on Kan'Varil.

"Well, if that's not perfect timing, I have no idea what is," Yulkii said after I passed her the spyglass. She passed the spyglass back to Xaddjyk who peered through it again.

"So can an army of Kalydiin knights defeat an army of samurai?" I asked in genuine curiosity.

Yulkii shrugged, bobbed her head slightly in one direction and then the other, and winced slightly before saying, "Yes, both sides have major advantages and disadvantages, but in this case the advantages held by the knights are greater. They have the superior numbers needed as well as battle mages, which samurai armies do not employ typically. With the greater numbers and mages, they could sweep the field. Also knights have a major advantage when it comes to defense. Samurai never use shields, as it is dishonorable. However, knights love shields, and they tend to give them a major edge in survivability."

"As such, the knights should be able to counter the samurai, especially since their army is pretty small. They will not attack Kan'Varil, but neither will they turn tail and go home. We should expect to see them again," Xaddjyk said.

"We still need to get back to Kan'Varil and gather everyone together, but where do we go from there?," I asked.

"I need to talk to an old friend. We need to discover why the whole world is descending into chaos and lawlessness. It all sounds too familiar," Xaddjyk replied. "We are heading to Aaomysiir, where we will finally discover what darkness is at the heart of all this . . ."

CHAPTER 7

SECRETS

I'm going to jump ahead slightly to skip past all the boring walking. Xaddjyk decided that we needed to return to Kan'Varil to collect the rest of our allies before moving on. We had to walk all the way back to the keep but ran into nothing interesting on our way back. Once we got in sight of Kan'Varil, I could see that the army of knights that we saw on the road had already arrived. They were camping within the breached walls of the fortress and had patrols out along the roads and in the sacked towns around the fortress. They were obviously informed that we were on our way, as they didn't bother stopping us. Once we made it into the wall we found another five hundred or more soldiers scattered about, pitching tents and making camp. Most of the structures in the fortress outside the keep were heavily damaged during the siege. We were allowed to move through the fortress without hindrance, and many of the knights stood aside and saluted as we passed. I'm guessing they were saluting Kara, not Xaddjyk, since she was the one with a rank, and a fancy one too. As soon as we got up to the keep, where the golem was still standing in the gateway with a dozen knights around it trying to figure out what to do with it, Xaddjyk pulled the Hammer out, and the golem again stood at attention. Xaddjyk went to dissolve their company and get them to leave the golem alone, but Kara and I and Yulkii too just headed up into the keep to meet with Kinterson and Halkiir and the others.

The great hall changed dramatically since the last time we were here. The bodies of the injured were cleared out, and the defenders formally on the line were now guarding inside the hall. There were a large number of refugees running around outside the keep and in the fortress center. They must have run to the keep before the siege to escape the marauders. Judging by the numbers, I'm guessing that most of the women and children actually survived though a lot of the men were conscripted into the military to defend the fortress. We passed the keep and headed down into the war room deep in the ground. In the room gathered around the table were Kinterson, Halkiir, Baron Kyal, Commander Danyk, and a highly decorated knight whom I didn't recognize.

"Ah, Paladin, Your Highness. I'm glad they were able to secure your rescue," the baron started as we just made it down the stairs and into the room.

"Baron Kyal, I must thank you for sending such capable agents. I doubt that anyone else could have accomplished that mission," Yulkii said, approaching the table.

"Princess Yulkii, Paladin Justicar Kara, this is—" Baron Kyal started before he was interrupted by the knight.

"General Graves, Royal Knights out of Aaomysiir. My contingent was dispatched a month ago to resolve the conflict in this region. It's sad that we arrived too late to save the fortress, though fortuities that you and your companion arrived when you did," the general said.

"General Graves, I've heard of you. I'm surprised that the king would send you on this kind of errand," Kara remarked, stepping forward.

"Paladin Prelate Kara, I too have heard of you, and I am surprised that such an illustrious Justicar would be among this company."

"We are heading to Aaomysiir, actually. We need to meet up with someone in an attempt to find the darkness at the heart of all this chaos," Kara explained.

"Well, I am unsure who you mean that could shed light on the current shit storm the world is experiencing, but at the least you would be welcome in the capital. The king has gathered his legions and is consolidating power around the isle. I was sent here because I am to take command of all forces in this region and to secure it from attack," the general explained.

"I can't think of anyone better for the job then you, General."

He nodded and said, "Aaomysiir is a far hike from here, five hundred miles. Is your plan time-sensitive, as I doubt you can make it there in under a month?"

"Xaddjyk is planning on using the Wayshrines," Kara said.

"Smart. I wish we knew how they worked, as it would make travel a lot simpler and quicker."

"Well, the problem is that they aren't active, but Xaddjyk will be turning them on, so you might be able to use them after he activates the network," Kara explained.

"I'd welcome that. I'll send a platoon of my men to secure the Wayshrine. If he can activate the network then that will give us a major advantage, as we will be able to move troops to wherever they are needed when they are needed."

"Talk to Xaddjyk. He understands the magic and the technology behind the Wayshrines. If anyone can attune them to your cause, it's him."

"You'll need a key if you are planning to make use of the Wayshrine, General," Xaddjyk said, appearing down the stairs.

"A key?" General Graves asked.

"Yes, when the Triaegis Empire built the Wayshrines they wanted to ensure that only their own people could make use of them. As such the shrines had two modes, unlocked and locked. When unlocked the shrines are attuned in such a way that they resonate magic between all the Wayshrines. However, they can also be locked either selectively or broadly, forcing the energies from the Wayshrines to require a specially attuned signal. This signal is attuned using a crystal key. I can lock all the Wayshrines so that only your men equipped with these keys can access the network," Xaddjyk explained.

"What do you mean by 'selectively'?" the general asked.

"It is possible to lock certain shrines so that they require a key to access either to or from while leaving the rest of the network open for free travel."

"Where can we receive these keys so we can distribute them where they are needed?"

"I can make them at the shrine, however many you need," Xaddjyk said.

"I will send a platoon with you to secure the shrine. If you wouldn't mind giving them some of these keys, I will have them distributed to the other generals."

"Very well. I will activate the network and lock the attenuator. I will show your captain how to use the Wayshrine, but we must leave. Who's coming? Anyone else can remain here or go where they need to using the Wayshrine."

"I'm going," I said, running over to the stairs where he was standing.

"I have to return to Windrift Fortress and report to the Sentinels. I am unsure what their next move is or if they want to mobilize more forces. Halkiir, go with Xaddjyk and Kya and learn whatever his source can tell you. If the information is important use the Wayshrine to report to Windrift immediately. Otherwise, I will find you at Aaomysiir," Kinterson said.

Hawk stepped forward. "Well, I'm with you as always, old friend."

"Very well, let's go," Xaddjyk said, heading up the stairs with us behind him. The Knight Captain was staying here with his fellows, and Kinterson was taking his Sentinels back to Windrift for further orders. We had to walk a good distance in order to get to the wayshrine. The Wayshrines were built by the Triaegis Empire during their golden age and have been shut down ever since the fall of their empire, and no one has ever gotten them to work. In fact most people, for the longest time, had no clue what they were for; it was only in recent years that scholars have discovered their purpose. However, most of civilization isn't built with the Wayshrines in mind, and as such they can be pretty distant from places you would want them. I understand that some sites, such as Aaomysiir and Windrift Fortress, were built by the Triaegis Empire; and as such they have Wayshrines integrated into their designs. Most cities don't have Wayshrines within them, but any city or fortress that was built on the ruins of a Triaegis counterpart will have one, as these things seem to be extremely difficult to destroy. Even after several thousand years and the fact that practically every structure from the empire has long since decayed or crumbled, the Wayshrines have held against time very well. The Wayshrine nearest us was something like five miles out from Kan'Varil among the ruins of an ancient outpost that dates back to about the same time that the other keep was built and was in far worse shape, and all that remained was the stone foundation and a few archways.

The wayshrine was somewhere in the middle of the fallen outpost and was pretty surrounded by two-foot-high overgrowth. It stood ten feet high and was made of dark stone. There was a large crystal in the center of the top, and there were four long stone claws around the crystal. There was a three-dimensional map on a pedestal that had small crystals that indicated where the other Wayshrines were located. This map only showed the continent and had nothing beyond suggesting that these Wayshrines could not access other shrines on other continents. From the look of the map, there were hundreds of Wayshrines scattered throughout Kaladiin'Aaiyyr. The shrine was dark and clearly wasn't on. Xaddjyk pulled out the staff that he still wore on his back and opened the key part of it and all three of the wheel bars. There was a small port for the key behind the pedestal where the key staff fit into. He wound the gears like he did many times before until the stone in the staff began to glow with a blinding inner light, which passed to the crystal in the wayshrine. The light in the crystal flared with a bright light that dimmed slightly but still glowed with a significant amount of light. He left the staff in the keyhole and returned to the pedestal and placed both of his hands on the map. His eyes began to glow bright-red fire as he channeled magic into the shrine from himself. After a few moments all the crystals on the map began to light up one by one as he activated the network. The crystal in the wayshrine was glowing blue as well as all the crystals on the map. He pulsed an aura of red energy that changed the blue crystal within the shrine and all the stones on the map to red. I believe that this meant that all the shrines were now locked.

Xaddjyk placed his hand on the staff and the stone on the staff, and the crystal flared several times, and the energy from the staff's crystal shot down the shaft of the staff and into the ground of the pedestal. A stone drawer protruded from the body of the shrine, and within it were several dozen clear crystals that had an inner white light. We had a platoon of knights with us, which was equal to thirty-two or so knights.

"These are the keys you will need. You only need one to unlock the shrine and allow you to transport you and a large group to any shrine active on this map," Xaddjyk said with one of the keys in his hand.

"To use it you simply need to have the crystal in your possession, and the resonations from it will unlock the shrine so long as you are in physical contact with it. However, there is a magical aspect required in order to use these crystals and the Wayshrines, so your battle mages will be required. You do not need to worry about someone stealing these keys, as they must be imprinted on a mage so that it becomes active. Imprinting it is as simple as a mage using the key on the shrine the first time, and it will become bound to that mage forever," he explained, tossing the crystal he had to the head battle mage that accompanied the platoon.

"What about those that are still dark?" asked the battle mage, looking over the map on the pedestal.

"Those are deactivated locally and can only be reactivated locally. This usually implies that that wayshrine is within an important imperial sight that they locked up during the fall in order to keep them safe and undiscovered. Those are not for you, and you will be incapable of accessing either through the wayshrine network or through direct access. It's best if you ignore them," Xaddjyk said, pulling the staff out of the shrine and locking the bars back into place.

"Take all the keys and have them distributed as you see fit," he continued, approaching the map pedestal.

"Uh, sir, don't you need one of these?" the battle mage said, holding it up.

"No, I activated these shrines through an act of creation. That act of creation has bound these shrines to me as the crystal keys bind to the mages that use them. Kinterson, you should go first. Take a key and touch the crystal located at Windrift. You will have to concentrate on everyone that you want to bring with you, or else they will be left behind," Xaddjyk said, handing Kinterson one of the keys.

"Xaddjyk, we'll meet again. You're not half the pain in the ass I thought you were," Kinterson said, holding his hand out. Xaddjyk took his arm around the wrist, and Kinterson did the same as a sign of respect. Kinterson then turned around and activated the shrine's map pedestal, and his key began to glow as did the crystal in the wayshrine and him and all his men disappeared. It was almost as if they were turned into energy and devoured by the crystal in the shrine. They all turned into a white light that flew into the crystal of the shrine, and it came to glow before the light flashed brightly and was gone. Xaddjyk was next, and he activated the crystal that was in the middle of Aaomysiir, and there was a white light, and suddenly we were in the center of the city.

We were standing around a wayshrine that looked exactly the same as the one we were just at, but the surroundings were radically different. We were standing in a wide courtyard that seemed to revolve around the wayshrine. The ground was tiled in white-and-blue rectangular stones that encircled the wayshrine in a large area around it. There were four large, spirelike structures around the circular courtyard made of the same white-and-light-blue granites. We must have been in the center of the palace district, as all the surrounding structures were tall and formed in towers and spires built of light stone, white metals, and crystal construction. The skyline was massive and stretched far into the distance and hid the rest of the city from view. It was fairly clear that this part of the city was constructed by the Triaegis Empire and was one of the only remaining aboveground constructions still intact. There was a collection of people around the courtyard who were all looking at us shocked at having seen the wayshrine active for the first time ever. Most of the people were wearing intricate clothing in a wide variety of vivid colors, indicating that they were likely of noble origin. There was a collection of armed and decorated guards around the courtyard wearing some of the fanciest armor I have ever seen before. One of the guards who had insignias on his armor, suggesting that he was a captain, with two other guards approached us from deeper in the city. As Xaddjyk stepped away from the wayshrine, the crystal in it dimmed slightly but still had a distinguishable inner light.

"Kara, you mind handling this?" Xaddjyk said, stepping back. Kara nodded and stepped forward to intercept the three guardsmen.

"Hail, friend. We received a rumor that five persons just appeared out of thin air in the courtyard," the guard captain said, reaching Kara in the center of the courtyard.

"I am Captain Bael, head of the guardsmen in this district, and who are you and how did you do whatever it was that you did" the guard asked.

"I am Paladin Prelate Kara of the Imperial Justiciars, and I am escorting Princess Yulkii Taa of the Chae Empire and Halkiir of the Sentinels. My companion Xaddjyk has just reactivated the ancient Triaegis Wayshrines, and we used it to transport her directly from the fortress at Kan'Varil," she explained.

"I'm sorry, ma'am. I was never informed that this thing was used for transport or to expect for foreign dignitaries of such prestige. Is there somewhere in the city that you need an escort to, my lady," the guard asked, bowing slightly to Yulkii.

"We could use an escort to the palace. I need to speak to King Adyus., It's important. However, I believe that my fellows have other agendas that require their assistance," Yulkii said.

"Yulkii, I will accompany you as I have a report to give to the king on behalf of the Sentinels. Kya, you should come too," Halkiir said, and Yulkii nodded.

"Very well, ma'am. I will send for an escort, and then we will head for the palace. Is there something that you need, Paladin Prelate?" the guard asked.

"No, guardsman. Xaddjyk and myself are here for nonofficial matters which need to concern the city guard," she said. The guard nodded and waved an entourage of guards that had just entered through a gate along the leftmost path.

"Kya, it seems like you are heading into another unknown situation. However, this time I doubt that we will be able to assist you if you get into trouble," Kara started. She shortened her spear by removing a foot-long segment off the bottom shaft. She twisted it and pulled it off, revealing three prongs that connected it to the main spear. The piece that she pulled off had the prongs but wasn't long enough to reach where the hidden blade was stored. The next segment of the shaft was the sheath for the inner blade, but by removing the lower segment she converted her six-foot-tall spear into a five-foot-tall spear.

"Here, take this. I will be coming back for it, so don't get too comfortable with it, and don't lose it. It may help you keep out of trouble, and where we are heading I doubt that I will be needing it as much as you will," Kara said, handing me her spear and the foot-long segment that she removed from the base. The spear was five foot four inches, which made it slightly shorter than me and quite comfortable in my hand. I stowed the foot-long segment in my pack, which fit rather well.

""Thank you, Kara. I'll try not to lose it although I have no idea what danger I will be subjected to in the palace," I said, stowing the lower segment in my pack.

"Actually, I have a small job for you. I need to take word to a friend in the city, an archeologist named Edwin Aldqiin. He has a store and lab in the main market square just off the central court," Xaddjyk said, handing me a sheet of paper that had the address on it and a bunch of writing that I couldn't read.

"I figure that you can handle yourself in a city this size, as you have experience with it. This city is dangerous, however, so don't lower your guard. To make matters worse, a lot of refugees and dissidents have flocked to the safety of the city as a result of attacks throughout the region. The king is consolidating soldiers here, so there are an abundance of guards and soldiers, but it's a big city," Xaddjyk continued before nodding and turning away toward the gate leading into the upper city. He pointed me to the gate that led to the city proper down from the old city where we were. The old city was located in the center of the island, which held Aaomysiir. The wayshrine was located near the center of the old city's lower quarter. There were four gates leading to the north, south, east, and west, to the other sections of the city. The eastern gate, where Yulkii and Halkiir were heading, led to the palace quarter, which was within a castle like Kal'Hinrathos. The palace and the castle were of the same Triaegis architecture and was part of the old city. The northern gate, where Xaddjyk and Kara were heading, led to the upper quarter where the wealthier lived and worked. It was a self-contained community with its own market district. The city was clearly not intended as such, but since most it was one of the only parts of the city that was left by the Triaegis, it became so. The western gate led down through the city proper belonging to the original Triaegis city. As I traveled further down the Triaegis city ended rather abruptly at one last Triaegis gate leading into a newer section of city. This part of the city was a stark contrast to the city I had just left and was clearly constructed by humans who arrived here after the fall of the empire. This was the primary part of the city where most of its inhabitants lived and worked. The southern gate led toward the lower city and Aaomysiir's factories and docks. The lower city was where all the poorer inhabitants lived, usually those who worked in the factories and docks.

Now I am unsure how the other two sides of this went, but mine was annoying. I headed through the western gate toward the city proper down several flights of stairs and into the more crowded part of the city. After a point, I left the white-and-blue crystalline architecture of the old city and went into the stone work designs of the newer parts of the city. The parts that the Kaladiian's built were made of a host of different stone types including red brick and gray granites. The buildings were far less elaborate than those built by the Triaegis and were generally square in shape and as many as five floors high but usually no taller. There were several towers that housed the city's garrison posts throughout. The closer I got to the city's market plaza, the thicker the crowds got and the more I had to push my way through them. I was still armed with Kara's very valuable spear, which I had to make doubly sure not to stab someone with it by accident. I made it into the thickest of the crowds within the plaza area and the most ironic thing occurred—someone tried to pickpocket me. It was sloppy work, and as an expert on the subject, that means something. It was a guy older than me, probably in his late twenties or so, who tried to grab at my pack from behind. Of course I reacted by grabbing the offender's wrist and dragging him forward before kicking out his knee and sending him to the ground. I then snapped his wrist, making him scream out, and I drew my sword on him, stopping his scream as he was now afraid for his life. Like Xaddjyk mentioned, there were guards on top of us within moments, rushing in. They had clearly seen what happened, as they didn't accuse me of assault.

"Ma'am, are you okay?" one of the guards asked, standing next to me. The other two who rushed in picked up the man, and he winced as they grabbed his broken arm.

"Ma'am, we will take care of this trash. We're sorry for the inconvenience," he said, bowing slightly and hauling the thief away. I couldn't utter a word, as it was so strange being on the other side of the law for a change. Once the guards left, I started to feel a tad more normal and continued on my way. I got another twenty feet before I realized that my palm was full of coins that I was unknowingly stealing mostly out of habit. I guess I was having a relapse of kleptomania and was stealing, which actually made me feel more normal though I decided it was best to not since the streets were filled with vigilant guards. It took forever to reach the end of the narrow street and enter the courtyard. I'm sorry, but the whole walk, aside from that stupid thief, was really, really boring, and nothing interesting happened.

Finally after an hour or more of walking and getting slightly lost at some point, I found his shop. When Xaddjyk said it was *off* the plaza he didn't say it was located in a back, obscure street. His shop was dark and looked empty and had clearly been here for a while. The sign that hung out from the door was dark wood that was clearly decayed from time, but you could still make out the name: Ancient's Way. I pushed the door open, and it was cloud of dust waiting for me inside. The shelves were filled with artifacts from long lost times and were mostly pottery, some statuettes, a bust of some random and obscure goddess, and thousands of scrolls and books. There was no one in the first room that I could see though the light in here was terrible.

"Hello, hello! Anyone working here or whatever?" I said, poking around, only accomplishing the creation of greater dust clouds and coughing to death. After poking around a little more an elderly man in dusty but rather richly made robes of silk and gold appeared from somewhere further in. He stumbled in with an armful of scrolls and books and pages and other things. He was mumbling to himself, which was kind of funny especially since he didn't even notice me. I stood quietly as he started putting things away and turned to see me standing there.

"Huh, who are you? What do you want? You can tell that fat, old, miserable bastard that the price is fifteen—not ten, not twelve, fifteen—and he can go to hell otherwise," he said, sounding like an old man with his attitude, but his voice was not nearly as old as he looked in the dim and dusty environment.

"Uh, what?" I responded because I had no idea what he was talking about. He stood up straight and looked at me, and his eye shifted to Kara's spear, which really got his attention.

"Oh, what is this? Come to sell, perhaps? This looks most interesting," he said, being far less grumpy and looking less old too.

"What? No. Are you Edwin Aldqwiin?" I asked.

"Yes, go figure. This is my shop. What do you want?" he snapped back.

"Oh, well, Xaddjyk said to bring you this letter and that you would know what it meant." He took the letter, reading over it quickly.

"Uh, isn't that disturbing? Come," he said waving me back into the next room within which he disappeared. There was a door but also thick curtains over the doorway. I had to push my way past the curtains, and within I found a large open room with tables and well-lit lanterns illuminating the room well. There was a larger collection of objects here in the process of being studied and cleaned or whatever.

"Well, this is interesting, but who are you?" he asked, folding the paper and placing it in his cloak.

"Oh, um, Kya. I'm Kya. I'm a friend of Xaddjyk. He asked me to come and give you that," I said, leaning on Kara's spear.

"Right. Any friend of Xaddjyk's, I suppose," he started before a rude and loud pounding on his door interrupted us. There was a voice saying something, but it was pretty muffled through the door though it sounded quite angry.

"Oh, what now?" Edwin said, poking out of the curtain, trying to get a better look at whoever was out there as well as better hear whatever they were yelling.

"Aldqiin, open the door! We've come for it and we aren't leaving!" the voice yelled while the pounding on the door got even harder.

"Ah, come on! These bastards never give up. Well, Kya, is it? I sure hope you are good with that spear—I doubt they are leaving." A moment later the pounding was replaced by them trying to break the door down. The door was solid and took the brunt of the beating rather well. Naturally the door couldn't hold forever, so Edwin grabbed a strange curved-edged sword, and he ditched the robe, revealing a rather simple tunic and pants that were covered in a significant amount of dust. After only a minute the door was broken off of the hinges, finally revealing our enemies. There were a dozen of them, and they were a real ragtag group. Though the leader was in a fairly nice set of leather armor, the rest of them wore patchwork clothing and whatever armor pieces they managed to acquire. The leader stepped into the shop over the intact but unhinged door, followed by his merry gaggle of morons.

"Well, well, Mister Edwin Aldqiin, shame on you. You never write anymore. Mister Takric'Baeu sends his regards and an inquiry about his package," the leader started.

"Yeah, well, I'm still waiting for my fifteen pounds of gold, which never arrived, go figure," Edwin said without hesitation.

"You received the agreed-upon price of ten pounds, and now delivery is requested."

"No, you said ten was an acceptable price. I said twenty-five and that there would be no negotiation in the matter. Twenty-five, you stupid, brainless oaf. So bring me my fucking gold or you will get nothing." Edwin was practically yelling at the group, clearly unafraid of them. He waved the sword around, making his point with it suggesting that if they crossed him he was going to cut them down.

"No more gold is coming to you, but the item is leaving with us. It must be taken over your corpse, and an old man and little girl will not stop us," the leader said, drawing his sword and losing all his fair demeanor and getting angry. All his friends drew their weapons though most of the weapons they drew were crude and rather crappy. The first attack was a surprise but ended up better than I could have imagined. One of the rear men charged forward from the line toward us. He was wearing some pieces of rough leather armor, such as part of the chest piece, gloves, boots, and half of a leg guard. His leather armor was in varying levels of quality, though most of it was in poorer condition.

He charged forward with a hand axe that looked more like a sharpened tool than a weapon. As he charged forward, Edwin was smart and moved out of the way, but I could not. I found myself stuck to the ground, unable to move, and it wasn't fear—it was something else something more powerful. Everything seemed to slow down almost magically, and instinct took over my body as if I was puppet. As he charged in, Kara's spear thrust forward involuntarily and impaled the man straight through the chest in between his ribs, piercing his heart. The spear slid into his chest smoothly and without resistance. The spear was so sharp that I felt I could have cleaved that guy in half with very little effort. After the man fell dead, I felt my body return to my control as if it was the spear that commandeered me, and now that the threat was gone, it relinquished its hold over me. Kara never mentioned that her spear was capable of doing this, though now I understand why she gave me the spear in the first place. After the first man died, the leader became very stern, and they all started toward me as a group. Edwin brandished his sword forward and was prepared for them to move it. His military stance was unusual and almost like Kara when she was using her short sword. He held the sword up with the blade diagonally downward and to the left. His right hand on the hilt was up high with his elbow being higher than his shoulder. With his left hand he held the un-bladed back of the sword near the sword's point. He was holding the blade more like a shield, expecting to block an attack rather than attack himself. The blade was single edged, and he held the broad side with his left hand, waiting for them to get close enough. If he was using the same stance as Kara then he was waiting for them to get into range, so he swung the blade down to the right and then up under the arm, cleaving the first almost in half. The leader waved in his men, and the remaining six moved in. Now the shop was pretty crowded, so they had to bottleneck in to get to us. At most they could attack two by two but no more. The first two headed in, and I could feel the spear taking over again, but through force of will, I could keep some control.

As the first man got close, Edwin did exactly what I thought he would and swung down to the side and then brought the sword upward under the first man's arm, slicing him open and causing his guts ooze out. The second man was clearly taken aback with the gruesome nature by which the other fellow was slaughtered. He moved in with a sword and a small buckler and was cautious about Edwin and his sword. He moved in slow and forgot about me. The spear bade me to thrust out, and like a good little puppet I did. The spear went through his shield, his arm, and into his side; and he made a squishy, gurgling sound before he expired. As I pulled the spear out, his blood erupted from his side and he fell over. The next two moved but had decided that brains would really help with this, and so the next two moved in with heater shields held forward and a third man behind them with a short spear and the last man standing back with a short hunting bow. I guess they got tired of dying and got smart about this. Of course this meant things were going to get interesting here.

"Stop this, Edwin! You can't win here. Give us the item or we will kill you!" the leader yelled. The sensation of the spear was getting intense, and it felt like it was vibrating in my hand in anticipation of the battle. It was warm in my hands, and I could feel an emotion from it like it was excited. It was weird. The two with shields moved in with swords held out, and the archer nocked an arrow. He fired his arrow, and the spear took over, moving itself in between me and the arrow, sending it flying. The two men with the shields rushed in, and Edwin swung at them, but their shields were actually pretty good, and all it accomplished was knocking the man back slightly. I decided to test this spear out thoroughly by trying to pierce through their shield. I thrust out, and it did penetrate the shield and into the man's arm, but I didn't have enough momentum to penetrate further. The spear disabled his arm and his shield which Edwin quickly took advantage of, swinging his sword downward through the man's neck and into his chest. As he pulled the sword out, a loud crunching sound preluded his death and partial dismemberment. The spearman behind the line thrust forward, trying to get at Edwin. He was still pulling his blade back and couldn't get his sword up fast enough and was pierced in the right shoulder. I was pulling the spear out of the dead man who fell to the floor when I had to duck to avoid an arrow that whizzed over my head. I looked, and he was preparing another arrow, and so I acted quickly. There was no way that I could get to him in time even if I could get the spear out of the shield in time, so I decided on another plan of action. I still had that crossbow that Xaddjyk gave me, and it was loaded with a bolt. I pulled it out, unlocking the rail and, with one hand, fired the bolt, hoping that I hit him before he was able to get me. The bolt slung forward and hit flesh, knocking the bowman onto his back even though the bolt only hit him in the shoulder or thereabout.

While I was still on the floor trying to dislodge the spear, the second swordsman tried to slice me. Luckily Edwin had pulled the spear out and with both hands rushed to the swordsman and got his sword in his chest all the way to the hilt. The swordsman dropped his sword, and they both fell to the ground, and I gave the spear one last pull, and it shredded out of the shield, and I went stumbling backward. The spearman saw me and tried to spear me, though as I said I stumbled backward, so he missed. The spear forced me up and forward and slashed the spearman in half with the blades on the headpiece. At some point around here, I was getting tired and sore from the spear pushing me around. What happened next was weird and actually painful. The spear propelled me further in a charge toward the archer, and I was able to bridge the distance very quickly. He was just barely getting up from the bolt I shot at him, and now he had me and the spear thrusting straight through him. The spear had such momentum that it pierced him all the way through. The spear had landed just under his heart and sliced a slash through him and tore free of his body out of his side. This sent the man swinging around as well as flying into the street. The leader turned to me and was ready to duel me. I decided that I needed every advantage I could get, so I started fumbling at the sheath, trying to get it off and get at the sword on the bottom of the spear. I did get it off by twisting it, and I dropped it on the ground, now having another blade with which to fight. I didn't need to know how to fight with a spear, as it did a lot of the work. I was expecting a good battle, and that's what I got.

He started attacking me, and all I could do was defend myself. He attacked quickly and I couldn't respond. I managed to get him to strike down and I pushed him away. I used the blade on the bottom on of the spear to stab him in the middle of his calf. I was then taken over by the spear and spun around, stabbing him multiple places with both the blade and the spear. Once the man was dead or nearly dead, the spear stopped controlling me. I fell to the ground. I was so tired and sore. Without the spear to propel me, I could barely move—I was dead. Edwin came out to get me, which was lucky since I had just rolled over and was about to fall asleep. I think I passed out a little, as one minute I was lying on the ground and the next I was on a dusty cot in the shop. I could hear Edwin describing the situation to a bunch of guards, and I can imagine that must have been an interesting conversation, especially given the gruesome nature of the attack. I was relieved that I didn't have to be there for that talk even though I still could barely move. I think I fell asleep again, as the next thing I can remember was Edwin, back in the room where I was looking over Kara's spear, and I had bandages on my arms, and my chest and my ribs hurt a lot.

"Hey, welcome back," he said, walking over to me. I was able to sit up though it hurt so bad. I was a little afraid I was going pass out again.

"Why does everything hurt? I don't remember ever getting hit," I said, stammering my words since it hurt so bad I could barely talk.

"You were hit—you had several dozen cuts, slashes, bruises, and you cracked two ribs," he said. I was about to try and squeeze *what* out but he got to it first. "It's the spear. It took over, and it kept you from noticing any injuries until the battle was over. Now tell me where you get this spear? It's not something one typically stumbles upon," he asked, helping me up and over to the table where the spear was sitting.

"It's Kara's. Not sure where she got it. I guess you'd have to ask her," I said again, stumbling to get my words out and passed the bouts of excruciating pain from my cracked ribs.

"Who's that?"

"She's a friend of Xaddjyk's. I figured you would know her." He shook his head and shrugged.

"How did the spear do whatever it is it did?" I asked, leaning on the table.

"This spear is unique and unlike anything I have seen before."

"What do you know about it?" I asked.

"A lot, though I doubt I know everything. It's unlike others of the same era. It is clearly of Triaegis design as determined by the construction. The weapon's design, primarily the headpiece as well as the extremely modular design of the weapon, is textbook Triaegis construction. The runes and details are also in their traditional design. However, it seems distorted and wrong. I can say that the advanced features, such as the modular components and the hidden blade, suggest it must be from near the end of the empire. However, the intricate nature of the weapon means it was from before their final war. All the weapons I have found that were made after the war began lacked designs or runes and were made only as weapons. The spear's all-metal shaft is a definite indicator of Triaegis design, as they almost religiously believed that wood did not belong on weapons. The strange part is that this weapon seems to have been made from the remains of another weapon. Both the remains and the primary spear seems to have been built for Avatars of the old order."

"What's an Avatar?" I asked.

"During the reign of the Triaegis Empire, they had Avatars that represented the greatest virtues of human nature. The Avatars were the ultimate embodiment of that virtue and are chosen from the order of knights that live to promote that virtue. There are orders designated to the virtues, such as valor, compassion, fortitude, justice, and honor, as well as others.

"Which virtue does this weapon belong to? Can you tell?" I asked.

"That's the thing I don't understand. You see, the white steel aspects of this weapon, such as parts of the headpiece, the inner blade, and the chains from headpiece, indicate that they came from another weapon originally. They appear to have belonged to a very powerful and highly respected Avatar of Justice. The most confusing part is that if she was so highly respected, why would someone remove parts of her weapon and incorporate them into another's weapon? Now the darker aspects of this spear also bear some of the marks that indicate the Order of Justice, but as I said they are distorted. If I had to make a guess this weapon belongs to an Avatar, but not one of virtue. These are corrupted and likely belonged to one the Deviants, a fallen Avatar. This weapon belonged to an Avatar of Vengeance, an aberration of justice. I have heard of Deviants before—they are rare, but sometimes an order needs to create an Avatar that can operate outside the normal rules of the order to accomplish a goal. This act is a mark of extreme desperation and, as such, is done very rarely. I don't know where Kara found it, but you need to return this to wherever she got it from and leave it there."

"Why what's wrong with it?"

"When a person ascends to the rank of Avatar, a special weapon is commissioned for them. These weapons are very unique and made for that Avatar only. After he or she dies or falls in battle, that weapon is buried with them. This is done because of the way these weapons are forged. They are made using a similar method as the Gauntlets. These weapons develop a personality as they are used, and they begin to reflect the nature of whoever uses it. This makes an Avatar's weapon strictly their own, and the essence of their being bleeds into the weapon. As this was built for an Avatar of Vengeance this weapon has the essence and personality of a powerful Deviant. This Deviant's will and hatred as well as their thirst for revenge have been imbued into this weapon. That is why it wouldn't let you fall in battle until your last foe was felled. You need to put it back quickly before whatever essence is in this bleeds into you or whoever Kara is," he explained

"Are you sure about this? What about the parts that belonged to the other weapon?" I said.

"They belonged to a powerful and quite famous Avatar of Justice as described by the details on her aspects of the weapon. The part that is a mystery to me aside from the fact that someone dismantled her weapon is how the two weapons are compatible with each other." I don't know what he read off the paper that Xaddjyk gave me to give to him, but it was disturbing for sure. I decided to sit down, as my ribs made breathing hard while I was standing, and he started gathering books from across his library.

"What was it that Xaddjyk wanted to do?" I asked, still sitting.

"He is under the impression that all the chaos that is brewing is a result of the Scourge reappearing. He wants me to cross-reference the current situation with that of the Triaegis Empire just before the start of their final war against the Dark Scourge," he responded, gathering a half dozen large and dusty tomes.

"He thinks that what's happening here is a prelude to the same event that destroyed the Triaegis Empire. He's wrong, right? I mean, that's bad—really, really bad," I said.

"Yes, really bad. We are not as united or as powerful militaristically as the Triaegis Empire, and if the Dark Scourge does return, we cannot face them with hope of victory."

"How did the Triaegis Empire fare against them?" I asked.

"Badly. They were able to delay their assault but unable to stop them. According to all historical data I have found, the Scourge first appeared here on this continent and moved through it and jumped to Januus'Anub and then Chaeyuun before landing on the continent that is now the shattered isles. Here the Triaegis lured the bulk of the Scourge's army and their leaders. Historical maps reference the shattered isles as a single continental body before the fall of the empire. Once the Scourge arrived, the Triaegis's most powerful mages combined their magic to create a massive vortex that consumed everything before exploding and destroying the entire continent. This trapped the Scourge in some kind of abysmal void."

"So, wait, they never made it to Valjjain (pronounced Val-hain), the continent were the Aegis Empire is?"

"Oh yes, in fact the largest section of the Dark Scourge's army was directed against Valjjain. However, Valjjain had an advantage that neither Kaladiin'Aaiyyr nor Chaeyuun had. Valjjain's emperor was often described as paranoid and overdefensive and spent most of his wealth fortifying the continent. Now most of Valjjain is protected by massive cliffs that prevent access from the sea. However, at the main entry into Valjjain the emperor constructed a powerful fortification consisting of thousands of miles of interconnected keeps, castles, and fortresses all into one super massive citadel. This massive fortification manned by hundreds of millions was known as Gray Haven, so named because the gray of the walls were visible for miles. Now Gray Haven is the largest connected fortification ever constructed and is fueled by the military might of an entire continent's military. The Scourge attacked here but were never able to breach into the walls of Gray Haven. Now rumors hold that Gray Haven's walls were guarded by more than just soldiers but by artificial steel soldiers. I can't speak to the validity of these rumors, but it is definitely possible. Now because of this, after the other two emperors became aware that victory was impossible, they decided to evacuate their empires to Valjjain. They evacuated their entire civilian population and all the military they had left using the Wayshrines, shutting them down afterward. This included the entire population of this city, which would explain why the Scourge didn't bother destroying it and just left it here intact. The military stationed at Valjjain included significant portions of the military from both Kaladiin'Aaiyyr and Chaeyuun that were evacuated once they realized they could not stop the invasion. They were hoping that their plan at the shattered isles would work at stopping the invasion, but if it didn't work they were planning to make their last stand at Valjjain," he explained, showing that he obviously had a lot of information involving the Triaegis Empire.

"So, wait, the Aegis Empire is actually the intact remains of the ancient Triaegis Empire?"

"Yes, though not much information gets out. They are isolationists, so practically speaking they may as well be gone since they won't share anything about themselves. Also we have no idea how much they have changed in the thousands of years since the Triaegis Empire fell. They went with the term 'the Aegis Empire' since they were one of the three major kingdoms which gave the empire its name. As far as I know only Xaddjyk and his pirate friend Dus'Pois have ever been there. They only have three cities outside of their borders, and they are heavily defended and do have the traditional Triaegis architecture though evolved and more advanced. The only three cities I know of that they still control is Tala'Vahnos, Tala'Mothae, and Tala'Kar. These cities were built to facilitate trade with outside nations without risking their borders to open trade. Tala'Vahnos is located on Chaeyuun, Tala'Mothae here on Kaladiin'Aaiyyr, and Tala'Kar in Januus'Anub. I made it a point to see them all, and I learned a lot about the empire, and it was in Tala'Mothae that I first met Xaddjyk." He went on to explain a great deal about the history of the Triaegis Empire, the war, the history of the time after the war up to more present times. He had a great deal of knowledge about a great deal of subjects, and as I have never had any formal schooling, this was great; and I learned a lot from him, and he seemed to like to talk about it.

There was a knock on the wood seal of where the door used to be hinged, followed by a voice saying, "Hello, uh, is anyone here? Kya, you here?" It was clearly Yulkii Taa's voice. I was still sore, so I was happy just sitting in the chair where I found myself.

"Back here," I yelled, remaining right where I was. I heard her and probably Halkiir navigating around the mess we created during the fight, and a minute later Yulkii swept the curtains aside and walked into the back room followed by Halkiir.

"Uh, what happened out there?" she asked, looking back out to the mess that Edwin's shop had become.

"Tax collectors," Edwin said without looking up from the table where Kara's spear and some other artifacts were located. Yulkii looked confused, but Halkiir got it.

"I'm sorry, am I missing something here? Why would tax collectors do this?" Yulkii asked, still looking back into the shop area.

"'Tax collector' is a term used typically by lower-society types to describe hired thugs. So why would criminal thugs try to muscle you?" Halkiir explained and asked.

"They wanted something and they didn't want to pay for it," Edwin said, looking up slightly and through the curtain that Yulkii was holding open. "Holy shit, they really want it bad." He stood up straight and walked to the curtain, drawing everyone's attention toward the door. There was another group of rough-looking men outside the door that looked similar to the thugs that attacked earlier. Edwin grabbed his weapon, and I jumped up, grabbing the spear. I was still sore from that damn thing and kind of scared to use it again. Edwin said that it wouldn't kill me, but I was unsure. I was in pretty bad shape the last time. Edwin pushed past Yulkii and Halkiir, and I followed him, getting ready for this again. This time was a little different, as the goons remained outside and only one man entered.

The man flung his hands up as he entered, saying, "Wait, wait, we are not here to battle. The men that attacked you last were doing so against orders from Mr. Takric'Baeu. We have brought the agreed-upon price for the item." He waved in another man, who was carrying a decorative box. Yulkii intercepted the man and opened the box to take a peek inside.

"The rest of the payment . . . you having received ten already," the man said. Yulkii opened the box and inside were several gold bars.

"So is it all there?" Edwin asked, still ready for a fight.

"Four five-pound bars of twenty-four karat gold with branding marks and label tags," she said, pulling one of the bars out to inspect the branding mark inscribed on the bottom.

"Fifteen pounds is what remains, not twenty," Edwin said.

"Yes, fifteen pounds is to complete the price and an additional five pounds for the damages and injuries caused by Mr. Odero and his men," the man replied. Halkiir took the box, and Edwin waved him back to the back of the shop.

"Very well. I have the item. Wait here," Edwin said, heading back. Edwin removed the gold bars from the box and replaced them with an old scroll wrapped in a cloth. He closed the box, and Halkiir carried the box back out to the men waiting at the door.

"Is this the item?" the man asked.

Edwin opened the box, revealing the scroll within before closing it again. He took it from Halkiir and handed it to the man who was originally holding it. The man nodded, and they all headed out and disappeared around the corner.

"Well, that was civil, sort of," I said quickly, heading back and putting the spear down. To be honest the spear scared the shit out of me, and I didn't want carry it around too long if I didn't have to.

"So what was worth twenty-five pounds of gold and the lives of twelve men?" I asked.

"During the end of the Triaegis Empire, after king Kalydiin decided that victory here was impossible, he started evacuating his people to Valjjain. The Scourge moved slowly, so there was plenty of time to get a significant portion of the civilian population as well as several legions of Kalydiin's military that remained after the civilians were taken to safety. A lot of nobles and wealthy merchants stowed their riches inside vaults to keep them safe, knowing that they could not take them with them as the evacuated to Valjjain. These were sealed with complex puzzle locks and encrypted cyphers. After the Scourge was defeated the wealthy nobles and merchants came back for their wealth, returning it to Valjjain. Most of that wealth aided in rebuilding the damage done by the Scourge that attacked there as well as constructing additional infrastructure to sustain the massive increase in the population. However, these vaults were no longer needed and were left sealed and empty. During the rise of man in Kaladiin'Aaiyyr after the fall of the empire, a lot of these vaults found themselves in use again. One such vault is still sealed after a powerful warlord poured wealth into it. The scroll contained the cypher needed to unlock the puzzle lock on the seal."

"Ooh, treasure," I said, smiling.

"Possibly, we shall see. Anything interesting he finds I will sell on his behalf," Edwin said, smiling at the interest of profit.

"Edwin, what the hell happened here?" Xaddjyk said, picking the door up and moving it out of the way. He was followed by Kara, who was carrying a large and rather old-looking book.

"Xaddjyk, my friend, welcome," Edwin said, coming out to greet him.

"Yeah, hey—but back to my question of what the hell happened. I mean you were always something of a pack rat but always a neat one."

"Tax collectors."

"Mr. Takric'Baeu."

"Uh, he claims it was against his orders, but who knows? He did pay five pounds for the damage, so I guess it's fine. Plus, we killed like twelve of their people, so now they know not to try that again."

"We?" Xaddjyk asked.

"Yeah, Kya really did most of the work with her spear, actually. She killed most of them, including the leader."

"What? Oh shit, she actually used Myrsjjal?" Kara asked, looking up, surprised.

"'Myrsjjal' is Triaegis for forgiveness, a weird name for a Deviant of Vengeance to name his spear," Edwin said, scratching his beard.

"It also means memory—revenge usually requires something to happen first, a bad memory if you will," Kara replied.

"That is really, really astute. Your knowledge of the Triaegis language is pretty good. I don't know anyone with your level of understanding," Edwin said, shocked and impressed, while Kara shrugged.

"Yeah, I used your spear. You gave it to me to use," I said.

"Ooh, I was hoping you wouldn't have to. It's fickle," Kara said, wincing. "How are you? Anything broken?"

"Two cracked ribs," I answered.

"Sorry about that. I honestly didn't expect you to need it. It was just a precaution."

"Well, it did save my life, so thanks for that," I said.

"Oh well, good, I'm glad it behaved for you," she said, continuing into the back room to get her spear.

I had a confused look and looked back to where she had gone and said, "What?"

"Edwin, we've got something for you. I believe this explains everything that's happening," Xaddjyk said, waving to Kara who still had the book, which she handed to Edwin.

"Whoa, this is a pretty rare to me? Where did you get it?" Edwin asked, already flipping through the pages carefully.

"Ooh, probably best not to ask that," Kara said.

"It's a rental, so keep it in good shape," Xaddjyk said. Edwin was quite interested with the book and was reading through it quickly, mostly skimming important parts.

"Wait, you believe the Dragonnaught is responsible for this? Well, that would explain a lot. However, I was under the impression that the Dragon Gauntlet was buried away hidden for all time. Quite frankly I have no idea where it was hidden, so I can't point you to where it was hidden to verify if it's still there."

"I don't even know where it was hidden. The Last Sentinels took it somewhere far away and told no one where it was buried," Halkiir said, shaking his head.

"The Dragonnaught Gauntlet was hidden near Aamurak Kor, deep within the Black Mountains," Xaddjyk said. Everyone was quiet for a time, and even Edwin was surprised about it. Now I have no idea what Aamurak Kor was, but the Black Mountains were some of the tallest mountains in Kaladiin'Aaiyyr, located near the border between Adiin'Ayr and Inuskard far in the north.

"The dwarves, why would the Sentinels take a powerful and inherently cursed Gauntlet to dwarven capital?" Edwin asked.

"Because the dwarves were who originally taught the Triaegis Empire how to build Gauntlets. It's hardly common knowledge, but the dwarves survived the siege of Aamurak Kor and still live in those mountains. As such they are the only ones who have firm grasp on Gauntlet technology even though the Triaegis modified the design several times since the dwarves initially taught them how to make them," Xaddjyk explained.

"I've never heard of this. Who told the Sentinels about it?" Halkiir asked, stepping forward.

"I did," Xaddjyk said.

"Well, that certainly proves you are more than meets the eye. That was a couple a hundred years ago," Halkiir said without sounding too surprised.

"If you think I am the only one who's older than six hundred years, you're sadly naïve. There are a great many people who have lived for several hundred years. There are several alive today, including Edwin who is two hundred and forty, and Kara, who is, also older than six hundred. In fact Aos was over three hundred years old when he fought Al'Maquise in Aaomysiir. Age is not a definition of difference, Halkiir. You of all people should understand that, being almost seventy," Xaddjyk said, and Halkiir simply shrugged in agreement.

"You are two hundred years old? Am I the only one as old as I look," I said somewhere between confusion and frustration.

"Yes," they all said in unison.

"Well, that's nice to know. Maybe you all can share the secrets of immortality with me. I can't say I would mind looking as good as Kara when I'm six hundred," I said.

"Well, thank you, Kya. It's always a pleasure to know that people think I look nice," Kara said, smiling and   looking around.

"Hey, I think you look nice, and I say so too sometimes," Xaddjyk said.

"I know, Xaddjyk, and it's always nice to hear to you say it, but you aren't really people in the common definition of the term, or any definition really," she said, smiling and looking over to him.

"Hey, that's, well, that's actually pretty true," he said, shrugging. "Regardless, in order to discover what's going on, we need to get to Aamurak Kor soon."

"Can't we just jump there using the Wayshrines? You know skip the walking?" I asked in general inquiry.

"Good idea. Unfortunately, no, the Wayshrines were a strictly Triaegis invention. Now the Wayshrines were difficult to construct and so only really built in places of high interest. The Triaegis never had many cities or fortresses to the far north. All that territory belonged to the dwarves' surface empire. If I remember correctly there were only four shrines near there. The first was located in the dwarven surface capital not far from the mountain pass leading to Amurak'Kor, but that city was destroyed almost completely," Xaddjyk explained.

"What happened?" I asked.

"Well, before the Triaegis decided to abandon these lands to the hordes of the Scourge, they tried holding against their onslaught in the hopes of either outlasting the invasion or devising a working strategy. However, as we all know, neither of those plans worked very well. The Scourge clashed upon the walls of Tor'Akal, the dwarven fortress where they were held at bay by dwarven defenders with the aid of two legions of imperial troops for eighteen months. Now the dwarves are the greatest architects that have ever lived, and their fortresses were believed to be indestructible and against anything shy of a limitless army they likely are. It was the defeat at Tor'Akal that led to the mass retreat in the first place. Now Tor'Akal was the major trade hub between the dwarven kingdoms and the Triaegis Empire, and so the empire constructed a wayshrine there to further facilitate such. However, the destruction of the city was so complete that that wayshrine will never function again," Xaddjyk said.

"Well, what about the other three? You said there were four near there," I asked.

"Well, one was constructed within Amurak'Kor for diplomatic reasons, but they shut that down after the war started and likely never looked at it since. Their wayshrine was different—it was constructed using dwarven magic, and though it connected to the same network, it functioned differently and so was not reactivated when I repowered the network. The third leads to one of the deep vaults and is likely sealed deep under the ground. Finally the fourth was built by Bastion, and he modified his beyond recognition, so I doubt it will function without some kind of key," he explained.

"So we're walking. That's great. I swear I never walked so much in my life," I said.

"Well, the walking is not so bad. Most of the territory between here and there is pretty peaceful. There are plenty of small villages on this half of the trip though things do get rougher the farther along we get. It may be a long walk, but we will grab some horses before we head out," Xaddjyk explained.

"Yulkii, how did your meeting with the king go?" Xaddjyk asked, turning to her.

"Ooh, very unhelpful. He is under the impression that someone is rallying the bandits here as a prelude to an invasion. He is clearly not going to help, and I doubt anything can be said to change his mind," Yulkii said.

"Go figure," Xaddjyk said.

"We should probably meet up with Kinterson before we head out. If we are going to experience combat on the way, we could use some more friendly blades. Also Hawk is always fun to have around, and none of us are marksmen, which is good to have in a group," Halkiir said.

"I saw Hawk on my way here. He is currently scouting in the woods but will meet up with us when we head out. As for Kinterson, he will likely be at the wayshrine with some guys hopefully. Also I took the liberty of recruiting some knights, and Kara got two of her Justicar friends, so we are pretty well formed," Xaddjyk explained.

"Wait, how long will it take for us to get there? The Black Mountains aren't exactly nearby," I asked, actually knowing something about geography.

"Well, there is a good distance between us and the fortress, so even on horseback it will take us a month, perhaps longer. Hawk will lead us along the Green Road, which will decrease our time considerably," Xaddjyk explained. We said our good-byes to Edwin and headed toward the wayshrine. Back at the wayshrine we met up with our group that was waiting for us, including Kinterson and three veteran Sentinels, two Knight Lieutenants and a Knight Captain, and two Paladin Justiciars.

"Well, it's about time you got up here. We've been waiting for some time. It seems you have arranged quite a group here—Sentinels, Knights, and Paladin Justiciars. It's almost like you are expecting trouble," Kinterson said.

"I like being prepared. You are the one that is always expecting trouble," Xaddjyk said.

"Good day, Prelate. We are ready to render assistance. I apologize that the order could not spare any additional forces or that we could not provide a full military escort. However, the Justiciars are spread out," one of the Justiciars said, greeting Kara.

"Greetings, Paladin. I'm just glad that I could get some aid from the order regardless of how much," Kara said, shaking the man's hand.

"All right, everyone has everything they need. We are preparing to leave. There is no turning back though. There are no Wayshrines on our way, so we need to take everything with us," Xaddjyk said.

We gathered our gear and headed out of the city. There were horses waiting for each of us, and some looked specific. Kara and her Justiciars all had pure white horses. The knights' horses were less specific, some being brown and others white. Xaddjyk's horse was a massive black horse that was taller and larger than the others, except Kara's, which was the same size as Xaddjyk's but white. They had a smaller white-and-tan horse for me, which was fine. I'd rather have a smaller horse, even if it was the smallest horse here. The horses were already saddled and ready, so all we had to do was hop on and go. There were a group of mules tied to the Knight Captain's horse, loaded with all our supplies.

I looked over the horizon as we headed out, Xaddjyk leading the way along the winding road and taking us into the north. Here we were surrounded by green and by life, plant and animal, but in the distance all I could see of our goal was the road and the faint outline of a mountain peak. I can't say how many hundreds of miles we would need to travel, but I knew our destination lay far over that horizon line. My journey took me from the sandy streets that I grew up with, the sand I knew and felt safe with, to a land that seemed otherworldly to me. Never have I seen so much color in the world as this, and even if we weren't so far from the walls of my home, it sure felt as though we had crossed into another land. Now here we were, headed so far into the north as to transgress an entire map so far north that we would pass into yet another world even more different than the one I knew. I don't know if I felt fear at being so far from the sands and the warmth of the desert sun or glad, glad to see a world beyond desert. It seems that no matter how beautiful a land may seem, beauty always masks a dark evil that threatens to devour the slow and slaughter the unaware. This was true in the desert, and it was true in the forests and plains we now traveled. The trip was like an insurmountable task that I knew would never end as we traveled with the lights of the great city at our back. With those lights sinking behind us as the sun set in the distance, I thought of the lights of Kal'Hinrathos.

When first I left the desert city and its walls and lights sucked into the distance, I was filled with deep feelings of loss and longing. I had a longing for the safety of its walls and the warmth of the desert sun. I expected this to be the same as the walls of Aaomysiir sunk away, and yet

I felt something different entirely. I felt a part of something, and I felt that even without the walls I was protected by those riding next to me. I looked back once more to see the city towers sink beneath a blanket of green grass before it was gone entirely, and I thought to myself, "I will be back, but for now I must look ahead." True, I have left two great cities behind me, but now I look ahead and know that another lay somewhere along this road. Somewhere far into the north lay the brilliant dwarven city of Amurak'Kor . . .